Text Classics

JULIAN RANDOLPH 'MICK' STOW was born in Geraldton, Western Australia, in 1935. He attended local schools before boarding at Guildford Grammar in Perth, where the renowned author Kenneth Mackenzie had been a student.

While at university he sent his poems to a British publisher. The resulting collection, *Act One*, won the Australian Literature Society's Gold Medal in 1957—as did the prolific young writer's third novel, *To the Islands*, the following year. *To the Islands* also won the 1958 Miles Franklin Literary Award. Stow reworked the novel for a second edition almost twenty-five years later, but never allowed its two predecessors to be republished.

He worked briefly as an anthropologist's assistant in New Guinea—an experience that subsequently informed *Visitants*, one of three masterful late novels—then fell seriously ill and returned to Australia. In the 1960s he lectured at universities in Australia and England, and lived in America on a Harkness fellowship. He published his second collection of verse, *Outrider*; the novel *Tourmaline*, on which critical opinion was divided; and his most popular fiction, *The Merry-Go-Round in the Sea* and *Midnite*.

For years afterwards Stow produced mainly poetry, libretti and reviews. In 1969 he settled permanently in England: first in Suffolk, then in Essex, where he moved in 1981. He received the 1979 Patrick White Award.

Randolph Stow died in 2010, aged seventy-four. A private man, a prodigiously gifted yet intermittently silent author, he has been hailed as 'the least visible figure of that great twentieth-century triumvirate of Australian novelists whose other members are Patrick White and Christina Stead'.

MICHELLE DE KRETSER was born in Sri Lanka and lives in Australia. She is the author of four novels, the most recent of which is *Questions of Travel*.

ALSO BY RANDOLPH STOW

The Suburbs of Hell
Randolph Stow

Text Publishing Melbourne Australia

textclassics.com.au
textpublishing.com.au

The Text Publishing Company
Swann House
22 William Street
Melbourne Victoria 3000
Australia

First published by Secker and Warburg, London, 1984
This edition published by The Text Publishing Company, 2015

Cover design by WH Chong
Page design by Text
Typeset by Midland Typesetters

Printed in Australia by Griffin Press, an Accredited ISO AS/NZS 14001:2004 Environmental Management System printer

Primary print ISBN: 9781925240313
Ebook ISBN: 9781922253125
Creator: Stow, Randolph, 1935–2010.
Title: The suburbs of hell / by Randolph Stow ; afterword by Michelle de Kretser.
Series: Text classics.
Dewey Number: A823.3

CONTENTS

The Suburbs of Hell

For WILLIAM GRONO

—twenty years after
'The Nedlands Monster'

Gasparo   You have acted certain murders here in
          Rome Bloody, and full of horror.
Lodovico 'Las, they were flea-bitings.

> *The White Devil*

Security some men call the suburbs of hell,
Only a dead wall between.

> Bosola in *The Duchess of Malfi*

But the demon, a black shadow
of death, prowled long in ambush,
and plotted against young and old.

Beowulf, tr. David Wright

In the Bible it says: *Behold, I come as a thief.* And: *The day of the Lord will come as a thief in the night.* That always seemed so strange to me, to find talk of thieves in such a place. And not in any condemning way, but dignified, almost understanding; which, when I first heard the words, struck a chord in me, being a thief.

In this little town where I find myself again, mist hangs unmoving in the few narrow streets. It is a winter day, at the very point when autumn is over at a stroke. Winter began this morning, with brittle light, air keen in the lungs. Across the estuary, which was calmer and had more blue in it than usually, woods and tawny stubble-fields had drawn close, showing details that at most times are blurred by haze. This special day of the year has a smell of its own as well: of chrysanthemum leaves in small hidden gardens, and of woodsmoke from the first open fires.

A thief is outside. He passes in the street, peers through windows without seeming to. He wants to be in, to handle things, to know. Lonely, one might think; wistful—but not so. A thief is a student of people, knows so many that his head is full of company. I have stood in a pub and seen a face, heard a voice, and slipped out and entered that man's house, calm in my mastery of all his habits. But then—ah, the thrill then, after my many studies; to find his things, his self, lying opened before me, all his secrets at my fingers' ends. For some thieves the excitement of that opening is a drunkenness. It is the intoxication of inside. Because a thief is, as he knows, an insider, a master of secrets. But the waiting may be long.

It is not envy or anything of hatred that brings me again to this little place in the mist which I have known so long and wished no harm to. I have no quarrel with the figures—uniformed in blue jeans and fisherman's jerseys, for the most part—passing quickly and alone in the dim distance. Nothing that the housewives prize, in the houses crammed cheek-to-cheek along the mediæval streets, touches my desire. I wish them well, or well enough, and their offspring: the divers from the quay, expert in flags and fish and sailings, whose sleep throughout childhood is agreeably troubled by foghorns and exploding maroons and the haunting sea. No; it is never hostility or malice. Simply, it is correction, a chastising.

In the mist, in the failing light, I pause before a door. He is never here, at this blue hour. The two windows of his large bedroom are open. I think mist must be wreathing above that lonely bed.

He has looked at me, several times, with a shy curiosity. Once I thought he was going to speak.

He is in a fury of resentment, in a gambling mood. He is undone by hurt. He has written to his brother to come and live with him. He will buy a boat, which he cannot afford, they will sail it to warm seas.

In the Bible it says: *Thou fool, this night thy soul shall be required of thee.*

1
THE MIDDLE YEARS OF HARRY

Harry Ufford woke in his armchair and removed from his lap his faithful cat, Rover. 'Goo and sit on your own self,' he complained.

An open bottle of whisky and a smeary tumbler were on the table beside him, and he poured himself a large drink and sipped it. The cuckoo-clock showed a quarter to nine. Drinking, he considered the room which he had now got exactly as he wanted it, the frame for his middle years.

It was a place full of ships and horses: of model ships in and out of bottles, china Suffolk Punches, and many horse-brasses. Over the fireplace, with its dying fire of coal and driftwood, hung a huge print of Constable's *Leaping Horse*, faced on the other side of the narrow room by Turner's *Fighting Temeraire*. Behind the glass of a bow-bellied cabinet were other knick-knacks, long in the gathering, also bearing on Suffolk or the sea.

It was a small room in a very small house, in a street which had preserved its mediæval outline and ran towards the place where the landward gate had once opened in the borough's walls. But Harry Ufford did not feel the narrowness. He had lived in a caravan, on ships and fishing-boats, and for an early year or two in a Borstal. What he felt was warmth and freedom, the privacy of his own special place, the comforting profusion of all those things, so lovingly chosen, which he had carried home to mark his patch. Harry Ufford, at forty-seven, drinking whisky he could pay for and smoking a cigarette of Dutch tobacco, from his usual matey source of supply, was at home like a cockle in the mud.

But the cuckoo would soon be out; it was near nine on a Saturday night. He glanced at the television set, at the bucket of coals by the dying fire, and, as he set down his empty glass on it, at the vivid paperback about sensational true murders. He was a devotee of real-life murder. But the forms of his society called him out once a week; and dutifully he heaved his large frame from the chair, stood for a moment in thought before the fire, then reached out a tattooed arm to a doorknob, and so made his way upstairs.

In his brand-new bathroom, the pride of his heart, he washed and shaved. In a brand-new mirror he faced his face. Broad-boned, still lean, a little flushed. He bent nearer to inspect himself, and with a fingertip touched a spot on the side of his nose, made up of little veins. 'Hot cobwebs, boy,' he warned himself. He ran his fingers, tattooed L-O-V-E

8

and H-A-T-E, through his black hair. It was thick and long, with no more than a spike or two of grey.

On his bed a cocoon of army-surplus blankets still kept the shape of him. He had no time for sheets, was not used to them. He changed his underclothes, and carefully fetched from the wardrobe some of his more formal gear. He put on blue Levis, a fisherman's jersey, a short black leather jacket. Over seaman's socks he pulled leather boots the colour of Ovaltine, with rather high heels. Then he paused to check on himself in a long mirror, while attaching his front-door key to a belt-loop.

He was in order. He wore the uniform of an Old Torn-wich Saturday night.

Level with his eye hung a photograph of his father, a very good one, taken by somebody famous in that line. It had appeared in a book, with the caption: 'Suffolk Fisherman'. A face lined and spare as driftwood, prickly with a few days of white stubble, the bright eyes among the weather-lines cautious, guarded, yet kind.

'You weren't such a bad old boy,' said Harry Ufford, out of the wisdom of his middle years. 'Sorry.'

As Harry was coming down Red Lion Street he heard, from the mist, a sort of hoarse shout, muffled, neither male nor female. Then plimsolled feet were running towards him, and a short body hit him amidships.

'Watch where you're gooin, boy,' Harry said, irritably. 'Whass that you, Killer?'

Killer was a twelve-year-old boy, and looked very tough. But his face, in the mist-muted light of a streetlamp, was not self-confident.

'Sorry, Harry,' he muttered, in an unsteady treble. 'Harry—'

'Did you sing out just now?' Harry asked. 'I thought I hear someone yell.'

'It was me,' the boy admitted, reluctantly. 'I seen something. I seen—I dunno. A thing.'

'What you on about, boy?' Harry demanded. 'What kind of a thing? A hooman thing?'

'Yeh,' Killer said, 'but—I dunno. I weren't expectin it, it give me a turn, that did. I was comin down the street, from this way, and I was goin to go down that passage, on the left. Then this—this person come out of the other passage, on the right, and stop for a moment in the middle of the street and look at me, and then go away down the other passage where I was goin.'

'Whass so special, then,' Harry asked, 'about this *person*?'

'I'll tell you this,' said the child, more bravely, 'that was something ugly. A loony, I reckon. With an anorak with the hood pulled up, and underneath this mask, the worst I ever seen. And hands with hair on, and claws.'

'Why, I sin hands like that,' Harry said. 'You buy them in a joke-shop. George Butt buy one, about a thousand years ago, for makin hand-signals from his lorry.'

'I int daft, Harry,' said Killer, with returning spirit. 'I knoo that. What I mean is, that person is mad. Out of his tree. Thass something I could feel, kind of.'

Harry stood reflecting, thumbs in his wide leather belt. 'I'll tell you what, boy,' he said, 'thass a joke that'll make sense to someone. There's four pubs he could have been headin for, gooin that way. In one of them all his mates are peein themselves just now. Or else he's disappointed. In this life, dear boy, practical jokes are mostly let-downs.'

'Are you goin by mine, Harry?' the boy asked.

'I weren't, but I shall,' said the broad protective man. 'I kind of envy you your imagination, young Killer. There int all that much drama in Old Tornwich. Yeh, I shall see you hoom.'

'There could be,' the boy said, defensively. 'Dramas, I mean—bad things. There's that many little passages and empty houses and dark yards and places where the street-lamps don't reach. What if there was someone mad among us here, in this fog?'

'Fog, he call it. This int no fog, boy.'

'All right, Harry,' said Killer, restored to normal, 'you know your way about. I always stick up for you when they call you a dozy prat.'

'I think you're lookin for a thick ear, doughnut.'

Companionably they turned into the passage, Harry's boots ringing on its flags. The stillness of the little town was stiller there, among high narrow buildings. The only light was from lamplit mist in the streets at either end. As they passed, Harry looked carefully into two pitchdark doorways belonging to empty houses. 'Now you got me started,' he confessed.

In the next street they stopped outside a small Georgian house. 'You carry a key, boy?' Harry asked.

The child shook his head, and banged loudly with a shining brass knocker in the shape of a dolphin.

'Well, I shan't wait,' said Harry. The reason bein, I have a dark suspicion your mam fancy me.'

11

'No,' said Killer, 'no, thass me dad what fancy you.'

'I hope you have nightmares,' Harry said, 'you perco-cious brat. See you.'

He walked on down the street. Through the mist the lights of the big ferry, the *St Felix*, shone bright and blurred. He stopped on the quayside to look at her.

'Great days,' he said to himself. 'Great mates, great fights, great piss-ups.'

He turned and walked on, beside the mist-breathing water, towards the sign of the Speedwell, dimly shining at the far end of the quay.

Inside Old Tornwich Speedwell, wearers of the Saturday night uniform were out in strength. Somebody's small dog was wandering, bewildered, through thickets of blue denim legs. Here and there the more formal uniform of a pilot added the touch of class which the Speedwell's landlady was always pleased to see.

'You don't get in much lately,' Frank De Vere said, drinking with Harry at the bar. The sound of his voice caught the ear of retired Commander Pryke, an irritable tippler, who turned to his neighbour and muttered in disgust: 'De Vere. Bog Irish by origin, and he's a De Vere.'

'Bog Norman-Irish, perhaps,' Paul Ramsey suggested peaceably, and puffed at his pipe. He and the Commander sat a little apart at a table by a window. Outside, the masts of a fishing-boat swayed unsettlingly in the mist.

'It come to me on my birthday,' Harry was saying, 'that my wild days was over. I said to myself, I say: Once a week is enough, boy, just to keep up the social intercourse, like. Well, I mean, at my time of life what you're fittest for is watchin the telly.'

'And I suppose you never drink indoors,' Frank De Vere insinuated. 'I suppose you wouldn't be half-cut at the moment?'

When scenting an offence Harry's face took on an odd expression, mild yet grim. Not moving his head, he said: 'Psychologically speakin, young Frank, you're a sort of a Peepin Tom. What the Frogs call a *voiture*.'

'*Voyeur*, you tool,' Frank murmured.

'Is that it? Where did I get *voiture* from, then?'

'Off the car-deck on the *Felix*, I should imagine.'

'Oh my mind, my mind,' Harry groaned, running a hand through his hair. 'Forty-seven, and my mind's in the state of an old Brillopad. Just you remember what I always tell you: this Abbot Ale causes brain damage.'

Frank emptied his pint nonetheless. 'No Dave tonight,' he said. 'Courting, I think.'

'Courtin?' Harry's glance was sceptical.

'Why not?'

'He never shew much interest before. Another thing about him: seem to me he have a surprisin amount of money for a young fella on the dole.'

'All right, then,' Frank said, 'he's out robbing a bank. You senile fucking *voiture*.'

Harry looked at him suddenly, really looking, with his jaw set. 'I think you're a bit of a nasty bugger,' he said, without heat. 'Sometimes I don't enjoy listenin to you.'

'Joke, mate,' Frank explained, uncomfortably. 'Here, drink that up, I'm waiting.'

While Frank hovered, trying to catch a barmaid's eye, Harry studied his own thick fingers drumming on a drip-mat on the bar. L-O-V-E; H-A-T-E. Those fists had got him into trouble in earlier days; the optimism and easy affectionateness of his nature turning to violence when he felt affronted. Now he was weighing up the case of Frank De Vere.

He could think of many favours which he had done for Frank, and for his withdrawn, unhappy wife. Favours, he saw on reflection, which he had rather thrust upon them; but that was his way, and people were used to him. If he had ever given the matter a thought, he would have counted Frank among his closer friends. But there was a matter of thirteen years between their ages, and it had dawned on him, after that sudden flash of malice, that this long pub-companionship was like the companionship of fellow-commuters, quite empty. If Frank sought him out, as in a passive way he did, it was because Frank was not liked. So (reasoned Harry) he get Muggins for his mate; soft-touch Harry, Harry the swede, that read a lot of books but get mixed up over the long words. Senile fuckin Harry.

If Frank had a real friend, though that would be putting it strongly, it must be young Dave Stutton. Yet Harry had gathered from the air once or twice that they did not much like one another. So what thrust them into each other's company so often must be business, after a fashion.

A pint-pot was placed between his hands, and he lifted it and said: 'Cheers.' He smiled his open country-boy's smile, not in hypocrisy, but because that was his way of dealing with friction, for a while. He did sincerely think the

14

best of people, till the moment when something demanded to be done.

Suddenly the mug's rim clicked against his teeth as he started. Someone had goosed him.

He swung round. 'Why, you naughty old lady, Ena.'

A bouncy little woman, bosomed like a bullfinch, stood beaming up at him. Old Tornwich knew her as Eddystone Ena: former ship's stewardess, former barmaid, and for many years the solitary tenant of an urban lighthouse.

As she opened her mouth to speak the jukebox, now surrounded by a knot of teenagers just come in, broke its silence with a scream, and he bent down to her. 'Hullo, stranger,' she yelled in his ear. 'Give us a kiss.'

He embraced her small plumpness, and kissed her on each cheek. 'Oh, isn't he a big strong fella,' she cried to Frank De Vere, who was looking down on the scene with his usual sardonic expression, eyes glacier-blue in his pockmarked face.

'Let me sit you on the bar,' Harry offered, 'where we can see you.'

'You put me down, Harry Ufford!' chortled Ena, enjoying herself. 'No, I can't stay, I was on my way round to speak to Doris when I saw you. It's the first time for yonks. When a man cuts down on his beer he just seems to vanish. You look very well, Harry. Younger, thinner in the face.'

Harry's guileless vanity responded; he grinned.

'Anyway,' Ena rattled on, 'you must come and see me some day at the lighthouse. We're neighbours, after all.'

'Will do,' Harry said. 'Thass a promise. But anyway, Ena, see you again before closin time, I hope.'

She passed, and he turned back to Frank, his equivocal mate. 'Thass a great little old gal,' he said. 'War widow, you know. She never had things easy, but always bright as a button.'

'You've been into her lighthouse, have you?' Frank asked.

'Oh, yeh, two or three times. She keep that quite nice. All her gear is shabby, like, but thass homely.'

'I and Dave have this fantasy,' Frank said, 'of going and knocking on her door. It would be a real Goon Show scene, we reckon. We'd hear her feet coming down a hundred and twelve stairs, then the door would creak open, horror-film stuff, and we'd say: "Is Fred in?" "Fred don't live here," she'd say, and the door would slam, and a hundred and twelve footsteps would go away again, into the sky.'

'I can see how that would appeal to you and Dave,' Harry said, 'gettin a woman with sixty-one-year-old legs down all them stairs. But she don't live in the light-room, as that happen. I doubt if she ever goo up there.'

'I'd like to see inside that place,' mused Frank.

'Well, play your cards right, boy, and you might get an invitation to tea. But if I was you I should prepare myself for it by thinkin of her in a more friendly spirit. I expect you noticed that you *dint* get an invitation just now.'

'Right,' Frank said, gazing impassively into his beer.

Behind Harry's back retired Commander Pryke, lurching a little in passing, bumped into him. He wandered on with a courtly mutter, and went out by the door on to the quayside. Turning at the interruption, Harry saw Paul Ramsey looking at him from his table, and brightened.

16

'There's young Paul,' he told Frank; 'I got something to say to him.'

He took his drink and went over to sit himself in the Commander's vacated chair, considering the bearded face opposite with benevolence. 'Well, young man?'

The beard on the young man's face produced a not uncommon effect, the line of the moustache making Paul Ramsey seem melancholy and resigned.

'Well what, Harry?'

'Well, whass that you're smokin in that pipe? That smell to me like King Henry the Eighth's bedsocks.'

'It's what I can afford,' Paul said. 'Unlike you, I pay duty on what I smoke.'

'Well, less not goo into that. There's some old customs in this place that a boy of your class and education don't want to know about.'

'You're fairly right,' Paul said. 'Bourgeois, we Ramseys are. If a policeman knocked on my door, I'd never feel easy with the neighbours again.'

Outside, the mist was thickening, and the bobbing, gyrating masts had become hard to see.

'Have you had a right rave-up with Captain Bligh?'

'He was okay,' Paul said. 'A touch of pepper when he noticed Frank De Vere. He objects to his surname—thinks it's far too good for him.'

'So that is. De Veres was great people in these parts once. The cream.'

'I could tell the Commander,' Paul said, 'something funny about his own name. But he probably knows it.'

'Pryke?' Harry pondered. 'Whass funny about Pryke?'

'A few years ago,' Paul said, 'I was going through some parish registers for a paper I was writing. In one village I found two families that kept intermarrying. Their names were Prick and Balls.'

'Oh, schoolmaster!' Harry exclaimed. 'Goo and wash your mouth out, boy.'

'It's gospel truth. The village was Boxford. In mid-Victorian times one family of Pricks started spelling their name "Pryke", and by the end of the century they'd all done the same. Now, if you look in the telephone book, you'll find a lot of Prykes, but the Pricks don't dare raise their heads.'

'I don't think,' Harry said, 'that your interests make you a very suitable person to have charge of the minds of our children.'

Paul looked surprised. 'You haven't any children—have you, Harry?'

'That was just a way of speakin,' Harry said. 'But I think I have. I might have. One. From before I was married, thass why I int sure.'

'You were married?'

'Well—not for long. The divorce went on for years, the marriage dint. But before that there was a gal what had a son I think was mine. I like to think he's mine. There's his name,' Harry said, pushing up his sleeve. Tattooed on his forearm was a red rose with a label across the stem saying PAUL. 'Thass why I like that name,' Harry confided.

Paul stared at the tattoo. 'You're full of surprises, Harry,' he said. 'What if it's me? Perhaps I was left on the doorstep of the bourgeois Ramseys.'

'Could be, for all I know,' Harry said. 'I never sin him. She wouldn't let me. He'd be about twenty-five now.'

'Not me, then. I'm thirty-one.'

'Are you? Blokes with beards, you just can't tell.'

He looked at the beard with such candid affection that the younger man sheepishly smiled at him.

'Do you know what I think about your face?' Harry asked. 'I think if I met you in the middle of the Go-By Desert, I should say: "Scoose me, boy, int you a Morris-dancer?"'

Paul spluttered into his beer. 'If that had come from any other man,' he said, 'I'd call him a bitch.'

Harry merely beamed at him, and shook his head. After a pull at his pint he asked, grave now: 'Are you comfortable in that old house of yours?'

'All right, thanks,' Paul said, sounding cagey.

'Thass something big. Draughty, I should think. Draughty as arseholes.'

'It's not too bad. Of course, it's not—we were going to take years to get it civilized. That's rather come to a stop.'

'Thass sad. Still, that happen.'

'I get the impression,' Paul said, 'that it's happened a lot in Old Tornwich. I've never seen so many deserted husbands and lifelong bachelors. I ask myself whether all these little pubs are cause or effect.'

'I think thass the sea,' Harry said. 'Seamen's marriages are often a bit dodgy, like.'

'I put so much into that old wreck of a house,' Paul said, and frowned down at a beermat which he was twisting between his fingers. 'I thought about it all the time. I suppose

I thought that we both thought that was the most important thing about us: that one day we'd sit in our Georgian house that I'd bought for a song and entertain our slightly Bohemian, mostly schoolteaching friends. When she was in the process of being swept off her feet by a real Bohemian, I didn't even notice.'

'She might come back, mightn't she?'

'No,' Paul said. 'I don't think that affair is likely to last, but she won't move backwards now.'

'Well, listen, Paul—'

Paul's eyes, looking up at him, were grey-blue and rather blank, or guarded. 'What?'

'Well, I mean to say, don't be lonely, you know—'

'No, I'm not going to be. I think Greg is probably coming to live here for a while.'

'Greg? Oh, the little brother. The stoodent.'

'Not a student now. Another unemployable Ph.D.'

'Whass that—Ph.D?'

'Doctor of Philosophy.'

'Ah, you're pullin my pisser,' Harry exclaimed. 'That skinny scruff with the guitar, you call him doctor?'

'I call him Skinny Scruff,' Paul said. 'So can you.'

'Well, they're rum places, these universities,' said Harry. 'But thass nice for you. I don't see that much of my own brothers, but we're pals when we meet. I should say for myself that I'm quite good at bein a brother.'

'I expect you are, Harry,' Paul said, with a straight face. 'If I met you in the Gobi Desert, that's what I'd guess about you.'

'Now you *are* pullin it,' Harry detected.

20

The big room, created not many years before from small ones which had been secretive and snug, was crowded and smoky by now, and conversations from many directions mingled in a throbbing hum like a ship's engine. The small dog was again navigating the legs with a lost look. 'Why,' said Harry, sitting with spraddled legs in his captain's chair and reviewing his fellow-citizens like a fleet, 'I believe thass Ena's dog, that.'

'You know everything,' Paul said. 'That reminds me: could you give Greg and me some advice about a boat?'

'To buy, you mean? Well, I know something, not a lot. But I can tell you who *not* to buy boats from. The hooman element, thass where I can always be a help.'

'Harry—what do you make of Frank?'

'Why, does he say he have a boat to sell? That can't be true.'

'No, nothing to do with boats. It's just that you put me in mind of people who offer to flog you things.'

Harry considered. 'I don't know all that much about him. We was both on the *Hamburg* once—we overlap by a foo months. And he stayed in my top room for a while, part-time, like. But I dint hardly know him then, and I don't think I do now, not to say *know*. When he get married, he come ashore and start this sort of handyman business: carpenterin and house-paintin and that. What are you tryin to find out? Do you know something against him?'

'No,' Paul said, doubtfully: and then: 'Better drop it. He saw me looking at him. He's coming over.'

Harry twisted in his chair and looked over his shoulder at Frank approaching. 'Come to join us, mate?'

'No, I'm off,' Frank said. 'I just remembered something. You're invited to a party, at Dave's.'

'At Dave's?' Harry said. 'I don't know where Dave live.'

'It's twenty-three High Street,' Frank said. 'A bit after eleven. Bring a bird, if you know one, and enough to drink for yourselves.'

'Well, I might,' Harry said. 'Shall I ask Ena? She always like a party, but I don't think a party of Dave's would be up her street.'

'Bring her,' Frank said, beginning to drift away. 'You're invited too,' he added to Paul, and then pushed his way through the crowd to the door.

'Well,' Harry said to Paul, 'shall you come?'

'I don't think so. If Ena goes, I might.'

'I know whass in Dave's mind,' Harry said, 'invitin us Old Age Pensioners. He reckons we shall get discouraged before we empty the bottles we bring. Stone me, boy, int you never gooin to finish that? What are you doin, spittin into it to make that last?'

'Just a half,' Paul said, handing over his pint. 'Harry, do you *like* Frank?'

Harry, standing with a pot in each hand, gave the matter his attention. He said: 'Thass not a question I often ask myself. I like most people till they teach me different. Far as I'm concerned, the whole hooman race is on probation. Nice to see you smile, boy.'

'Prat,' said Paul. 'Soppy prat.'

At the end of the quay the mist was thrumming with the engines of the unseen *St Felix*, and the streetlamps, reduced to dandelion-balls of light, made islands to be crossed by the dark sudden figures of men going home from the dozen pubs of the little town.

'I always think,' said Ena, tripping along in her court shoes with her King Charles spaniel behind her, 'they could make a spooky film in Old Tornwich when it's foggy.'

'Oh, yes,' Paul said, cheered up by the thought. 'Nineteen-forties. Black and white. With—'

'Basil Rathbone,' Ena suggested. 'Lon Chaney.'

'I was thinking of Jean Gabin.'

'Oh, foreign,' Ena said. 'Yes, and Valli.'

'Boris Karloff,' Harry contributed. 'Bela Lugosi.'

'I think we were being more subtle,' said Paul.

'There's a monster about tonight,' Harry said, taking no offence. 'Young Killer—Jimmy Rigg—see him in the next street. Some bloke in a joke-shop mask, with them hands—you know? The sight of that in the mist redooce Killer to a twelve-year-old boy.'

'Someone rehearsing for the Carnival,' Ena said. 'What was the number of the house, Harry?'

Harry wrinkled his brow, and gave it up. 'I forget. Do you remember, Paul?'

'I didn't hear him.'

'I should have known better,' sighed Ena.

'No,' protested Harry, 'we shall find it. If we wait, we shall see other people arrivin.' He came to a stop under a streetlamp, bottles cradled in his arms. 'Just you have patience, Ena.'

'It's not very warm,' Ena pointed out. She picked up her small dog and swept it to her bosom, and they nuzzled one another. 'Choochy features. Oh, she's shivering.'

23

Paul said: 'Do you think Frank was having a little joke? That there isn't a party?'

'No, I don't think,' Harry said shortly. 'Bloody hell, boy, he's a bit older than ten.'

'Here's a taxi slowing down,' said Ena. 'It must be near here.'

The taxi came to a stop by the light, but no door opened. After a moment a voice called from its darkness: 'Harry—you lost?'

'Whass that you, Sam?' Harry called back, and leaned in at the passenger window. 'We're lookin for a party, but thass hidin. Do you know where that is?'

After a pause for thought, the voice replied: 'No, but I know where there *is* a party. In New Tornwich. I'll take you there.'

'We can't do that,' Ena objected. 'Gatecrashing parties at our age—don't talk so daft, Sam.'

'That's all right,' promised the invisible driver. 'That's okay. She told me to bring people to her party. It's a girl I know what's celebratin her birthday, on the spur of the moment, like.'

'Well, I don't know, I'm sure,' said Ena. 'I wonder if she's got the police out scouting for her as well.'

'Is this sort of thing common in Tornwich?' Paul wondered.

'That's not *un*common,' said the voice of Sam.

Harry made a decision and, opening a rear door, stood waiting. 'Come on, Ena. If we don't fancy it, Sam will drive us straight home.'

'Oh well,' said Ena, 'why not?' She clutched her dog close and climbed into the car, Harry crowding behind her.

24

No one was listening to Paul excusing himself from the unknown girl's party, and after a moment he surrendered and got in beside the driver. He was surprised to find that Sam, who had the voice of a native of Ipswich, was a young black man. They nodded to one another, and Sam set off.

Once past Ena's lighthouse they were in the Victorian sprawl of New Tornwich, but the mist, stained by the crude lights of the main road, had made the houses retreat and become country hedgerows. Soon the taxi turned and crossed a railway line, and pulled up before a row of working-men's cottages of clammy red brick, where an open front door spilled light and disco music.

As the passengers were getting out, a blonde girl in jeans emerged from the house. 'Who have you brought me, Sam?' she called. 'Why, *Harry*!' She ran forward and was clasped to the black leather jacket with its perfume of good contraband tobacco.

'Donna,' Ena exclaimed. 'I didn't know it was *your* party. Happy birthday, love, give us a kiss.'

While the women embraced, Paul edged nearer to Harry. 'I don't think I'll come in,' he muttered. 'Not in the mood. Anyway, I'm expecting a phone call from Greg about midnight, I'd forgotten that.'

'Who is *he*?' Donna asked, discovering Paul. 'He looks nice.'

'He's a very nice boy,' Harry said, '(Paul–Donna), but he have to goo to bed early, so Sam's takin him home.' And while the women cajoled and Paul hedged, he opened the passenger door and slipped a half-bottle of whisky on to the seat, with a finger to his lips for Sam's benefit.

'Where does he live?' Sam asked.

'In Watergate. Fred Heath's old house. He's doin a lot of work on that.'

'He *bought* it?' Sam marvelled. 'Bloody hell. Even if I was a squatter, I should think twice about livin in that place.'

'Thass goonna be most desirable,' Harry said, 'if the poor lad don't lose heart.'

He reached out a black leather arm to Paul, who had come near, and crushed him to his side. 'You'll be all right,' he said, 'won't you. Now, look, there's a little bottle there, and you've to take that hoom with you. Ena and me int goonna spend long with these youngsters. We might come round to yours for a nightcap.'

'Right,' Paul said. 'Fine.'

'So don't you sit broodin. Your friends are on the way.' He held the slighter man for a moment in a bearhug, then pushed him into the taxi and slammed the door.

'You're crazy,' Paul said, laughing, looking up at him. 'You kissed me.'

'Did I?' said Harry. 'Well, worse things happen at sea. Look at him, Sam, don't he look like Don Quixotey when he smile?'

The taxi drew away, its tail-lights faded to ash in the mist. Broad-shouldered Harry turned and made his way, massive in the bright doorway, to the party.

Even now I curse the day—and yet, I think,
Few come within the compass of my curse—
Wherein I did not some notorious ill:
As, kill a man, or else devise his death...

Aaron in *Titus Andronicus*

The cellars are swept and whitewashed, cleansed of history. A setting that seems to call for casks and hogsheads and bales contains only the bland lumber of middle-class young people in their marriage's first scene.

The stairs creak. On the ground floor he has installed a fitted kitchen, very new, very shiny, nowadays not so clean. In the big dining-room with two windows on the street he has restored the old panelling and hung insignificant paintings, some of forebears of his own who could not afford to be painted well.

The staircase from there is of solid oak, carpeted, and does not give. On the first floor the door of his dark bedroom is ajar, but the sitting-room door, with light showing below it, is closed on the sound of the World Service News.

The stairs to the floor above are bare, and squeak. The rooms here are large, dingy, untouched; the windows are dusty. Nothing is here but the litter of his nest-building, rolls of wallpaper, tins of paint.

The one closed door below fits badly but has well-oiled hinges. He hears nothing through the News.

He sits listening, sprawled in a chair with his legs out, his head back, his eyes on the ceiling. He lifts a hand and sips from a glass. On a table behind him, near the window, stand the telephone and the lamp which is the only light. He waits for the telephone to ring.

In this room is much of his past, in the form for the most part of books, prints, records. It is the room of a student with money, a student grown a little older. He has not had an eventful life.

He has sat in this chair (crouched, rather) with his head in his hands, many a night. One night he took out of its case an old cut-throat razor with a bone handle, and stared at it.

But now he is calm; now he smiles at a recent memory. He waits for the telephone to ring.

And now I am inside; I know everything.

A movement, a sound, drags him back from his thoughts to the room. His eyes widen, he starts upright in the chair. He looks, through the narrow crack of the doorway, into my face, which he cannot see.

His eyes are on the one eye of the rifle. His mouth splits open his brown beard. He throws up a hand, palm outward, in an unwilled, futile gesture to ward off death.

2

THOUGHTS AND WHISPERS

At half-past six on a black Sunday evening, with the sound of bells being blown from the high spire over sea and estuary, Harry Ufford came wandering, hands in pockets, down the street, and at last stamped his cold feet to a halt at the edge of the quay. A light, biting breeze was up, but the black water was glossy, reflecting the lights of buoys in the channel. At one point on the other shore was a cluster of yellow-lit buildings, but otherwise a darkness of wood and field loomed unbroken against a navy-blue sky striped with ragged black cloud.

A slight man with a stick, standing in the same attitude further along the quay, turned to look at the heavy figure in the donkey-jacket, then began to move towards it. From a distance, he said quietly: 'Harry.'

'What?' growled Harry, staring with lowered head into

the water. Then, with a wrench of his neck: 'Oh. How do, Commander.'

In the hard light from the streetlamps the Commander's pink face was grimly sober.

'This is a terrible business, Harry,' he said. 'Frightful.'

'Yeh,' muttered Harry.

'I can't take it in. Such a quiet, harmless chap—'

'Thass not much to say for a man,' Harry said. 'But yes, he was a quiet, harmless chap. Mild as milk, as they say.'

'The poor boy,' the Commander said, 'the brother, he was in a hell of a state. He found him, of course, as I suppose you know. He had his own key. Came running across the street and beat on my door, asking to use my telephone. There was a telephone in the room, but—he wasn't thinking very well, needless to say.'

'You wouldn't,' Harry said, clenching and unclenching his dangling hands.

A pilot launch glided by, almost soundlessly, on the smoothly swelling water mirroring its red and white lights.

'If I knoo who that was,' Harry said, in a low voice, 'I should tear his fuckin head off with my bare hands. That int just talk, neither.'

The Commander moved a little nearer and, leaning on his stick, of which he had no real need but which he took for walks like a dog, looked at him with a sort of respect. 'You knew him better than I did, of course.'

'I dunno that I did,' said Harry, brooding. 'Just used to pass the time of day. I used to tease him, like. He was that serious. But he could laugh at himself. He was a good lad.'

'He was,' said the Commander sincerely. 'When my

wife was near the end, and I sometimes thought that things were getting on top of me, he and Diana were very good, wonderfully good.'

'He would be,' Harry said, but sounding absent. 'Oh Christ, Commander, what *is* gooin on? If ever a man would have wanted to slide out of the world with no fuss, Paul was that kind. But the mess—the rumours. Do you know what the rumours are sayin? They're pointin the finger at young Greg—his own brother.'

The Commander, giving a slight start, muttered: 'The sods,' in a voice quiet with anger. Then, more loudly: 'But that's utterly ridiculous. He didn't arrive here from London until eleven o'clock that morning, and I suppose he can prove that.'

'I hope he can,' Harry said. 'But if he want to convince Old Tornwich, he might have to goo into a dozen pubs and argue his case in each one.'

'Oh, that's foul,' the Commander burst out. 'Vicious. Don't forget, I saw that youngster that morning. He was shattered, utterly shattered, and crying like an hysterical child. My God, if that's a sample of the mind of Old Tornwich—'

'There is,' Harry said slowly, turning to look the Commander in the eye at last, 'someone else I overheard a rumour about.'

'Oh?' said the Commander, though clearly not anxious to learn. 'Who?'

'Me,' said Harry.

'I suppose that's a joke you'll explain,' the Commander hoped.

'What give rise to it,' Harry said, 'was something you told the police. That you heard someone knockin on Paul's door about half-twelve.'

'Well, yes, I did,' the Commander confirmed. 'Are you saying that was you?'

'As it happen,' Harry said. 'Oh, don't worry, the police know about it. So do everybody else. What it was, Ena and me told him we'd drop in on him for a nightcap about that time, but when Ena got to her own door she decided she dint fancy it. So I went on alone and give him a knock. Which you heard.'

'Well, dammit, Harry,' said the Commander, 'there's not much food for rumour in that. I was in bed, I heard a couple of knocks on the door across the way, that's all there was to it.'

'You dint hear the door open?'

'No. Well, it *didn't* open, did it?'

'No; but can you swear to that?'

The Commander shifted his stick, uneasily. 'Of course I can't. I didn't even hear your footsteps, either coming or going. I can't swear to a thing, except the knocks.'

'You see,' said Harry moodily, 'what it's gonna be like.'

The train of the conversation was restoring to the Commander his normal uncertain temper. 'I've never heard anything so ridiculous. If people are really saying this sort of thing (which, if you'll forgive me, I take leave to doubt) then their fascination with other people's affairs has driven them over the edge at last. They might as well suspect *me*. Perhaps they do.'

'P'rhaps,' said Harry, noncommittal. 'Or Ena, less say.'

'*Ena*? Good heavens, man.'

'I'm just puttin the case. Paul was expectin her. He dint hear me knock—he was in the bathroom or something—but he hear Ena, later, and let her in. There's a bell as well as a knocker. You wouldn't have heard that.'

'And—don't tell me—she was carrying a .22 rifle in a rather large piece of knitting, which she easily explained away.'

'Thass funny you should think of something like that,' Harry said, giving a sidelong look, 'because I hear a mention of something similar. Not knittin, but a roll of old charts or something that you took over there for him to look at when he was daydreamin about bein a yachtsman in the sun.'

The Commander's face became fierce and still. 'You have heard a mention of that? To the police?'

'Whether to the police or not,' said Harry, 'I couldn't say, but I did hear it crop up in a conversation, among the other theories. But I'm sure there's nothing for you to worry about, Commander. There's a suspect whass a much hotter favourite than you, or even me, and I feel sorry for that boy. I'm talkin about Black Sam, the taxi-driver.'

'Black,' said the Commander. 'Yes, I see.'

'You get the picture. Paul has a bottle of whisky with him, Black Sam makes a remark on it, Paul invite him in for a bit of a warm that cold night—'

'And, only pausing to stuff a rifle down his trousers, in Sam goes, I suppose.'

'No, think it out, Commander, like some of your fellow-citizens. Sam goo in, knock back a whisky, and say to Paul, he say: "Right, boy, thanks for the drink, I must now be gooin. Don't you get up, I shall slam the door on myself." And he make a sound as if he do slam it, but what really happen is, he goo to his taxi, get the rifle out of the boot and creep back in again.'

The Commander made an exasperated sound, and demanded: 'Is anyone idiot enough to believe that? What conceivable motive could he have?'

'No motive. His motive is, he's black. Mau Mau in the blood, or something like that. Thass the thinkin.'

'I am speechless,' said the Commander, dealing a blow at his own leg with his stick. 'I've spoken to that young chap, more than once. He was born and bred in Ipswich, and his parents came from Antigua. "Mau Mau in the blood", indeed.'

A few quarrelsome gulls rose from the water near the brightly lit *St Felix* and wheeled screaming overhead. Harry put back his head to look at them. When he spoke again, it was in a mourning tone.

'He was very quiet all his life,' he said, 'and he did no one in the world a bad turn. He was good to his brother and good to his wife, except in some way we can't know. P'rhaps we shall know now; everything's open now, for everyone to pass judgement on. All his things that he put together to make a home for himself in the world, all that's open for everyone to finger or blow fingerprint-dust over. When he was alive he dint do nobody no harm; and now he's dead, he's goonna tear this place apart.'

He drew the back of his hand across his mouth and sniffed against it.

'I must now be gooin. Sorry if I talked too much, Commander. I'm a bit upset, and a bit—murderous, like, today. It was listenin to the bells and thinkin: "This is the second Sunday he's been dead."'

The Commander came closer and laid a hand on his arm. 'I'm sorry too, Harry, if I sounded impatient with some of the kites you were flying.'

'That int me whass flyin 'em,' said Harry, turning away. 'You'll find that out for yourself at the first pub you goo into. Commander, this little old town of ours is in the buggeredest muddle.'

Eddystone Ena came bustling out of the smart new kitchen, which delighted and overawed her, with a tray clutched beneath her pouting little bosom, and went into the panelled dining-room at the front of the house. She set down the tray on the large shining table, then went out again into the passage, where a door stood ajar. She knocked softly before pushing it open.

'Greg,' she said, tentatively.

The head of a young man who was stretched out on a sofa inside a blue sleeping-bag turned on a pillow to look at her. 'Yes, Ena?'

'I ignored you, and cooked some supper for you. Be a good boy and come straight away, before it's cold.'

'Right,' Greg Ramsey said. 'Thanks.' He worked his legs out of the sleeping-bag and stood up, thin in denim jeans and jacket and a tee-shirt with a conservationist slogan. His general cut was hippyish and his sandy hair long, but he was cleanshaven except for a heavy blondish moustache curving around a mouth with a childish fullness of the lips.

'Did you sleep?' Ena asked.

'No,' he said. 'But I will. I do. I've got some pills to take.'

He followed her into the dining-room and let her edge him towards a chair, and watched her place in front of him a large plate of scrambled eggs on toast. 'Just light,' she said. 'Now I'll bring mine in, and the tea. I thought it would be nicer if I kept you company.'

While she was out of the room he rested his head on one hand and fingered the stains of weariness under his eyes. But he had dropped his arm, and brightened, by the time she returned.

Attending to her own meal she exclaimed, with an innocent pleasure she would not have dreamed of concealing: 'Oh, isn't this nice.' The niceness was in the furniture of the room and the objects on the table: relics, for the most part, of the Ramsey parents, modest members of the upper bourgeoisie. 'If you could have seen this house when old Fred Heath owned it.'

'I did see,' Greg said. 'Well, I saw it soon afterwards. It was a mess. Ena, why do you live in a lighthouse?'

'Well, I didn't have very much choice,' said Ena, pouring tea. 'Things were so difficult after the war, what with bombing and floods and these old, old places simply falling down into the streets. Elizabethan houses, and even houses from the Middle Ages, like Commander Pryke's, over there. Oh, should I have drawn the curtains?'

'It doesn't matter,' Greg said. 'By now I feel I've been living in the market-place for ever.'

'The streets are very quiet,' Ena said, 'except for the High Street. What was I saying? Well, I had an uncle who

36

lived in the lighthouse. He leased it, you know, from the Borough Council; had been there for donkey's years, but was quite old and needed a different sort of place. So, I found him one, and I moved into the lighthouse with my boy Winston. He loved it, poor lamb. It made him interesting to the other lads at school. They were always coming to call.'

'He's grown-up now,' Greg supposed. 'Well, of course.'

'Oh, how time does fly,' said Ena. 'He would be thirty-seven this year. I can hardly believe it. But he passed away, poor little love, when he was ten. Polio.'

The young man pushed his plate away, and emptied his cup. 'I'm sorry I brought it up. Really I am, Ena.'

'Now I've made you feel awkward,' Ena said, a sincere apology. 'After all these years I talk about him without thinking that other people won't know what to say. I suppose I've never taken it in. Oh, you've eaten everything, you good boy.'

He was brooding over what she had said, hands gripping the table's edge, eyes staring into the shining wood of it. He said, with wonder: 'Someone has murdered my big brother. Someone carefully aimed a gun at him and made a hole in the middle of his forehead. It's incredible. I don't believe a word of it.'

'Now, Greg,' Ena said. Years of earning her living behind bar-counters had given her a sort of facility in soothing men who felt disgruntled or hardly used; but the light touch she had cultivated then could not be called on here. She came beside the young man and laid a hand on his shoulder. 'It's always so hard to credit, at first, but in the end you do. In the end, you remember the best things.'

'He was more like,' Greg said, 'more like a young uncle than a brother, because of the age-difference. Our parents were killed in a car accident, I suppose you've heard that, when he was eighteen and I was eleven. He's always made everything easy for me. I wonder if there were money worries. I wonder if it was for my sake that he took on such a boring career.'

'Oh, you mustn't say that,' Ena protested. 'It's not fair to him. He loved being a schoolteacher. It's what he was made for.'

'Yes,' he said, while she stroked his head. 'I beg his pardon. He knew what he was doing.'

'Your hair's so rough,' said Ena critically. 'I think I shall bring you some of that new conditioner that I use myself.'

He gave a little choking laugh, and looked round at her. 'Thanks,' he said. 'It's okay now, Ena. I'm believing it again.'

She went back to her chair, sipped at her tea, and found it cold. 'Greg, I don't like to think of you being alone here. I'd even rather you went on staying at the Speedwell, though it must be so noisy.'

'I didn't mind,' he said. 'I liked the noise. I hope I didn't hurt the feelings of all the kind people, like the Commander, who wanted to put me up. But I really felt better upstairs in a noisy pub.'

'But tonight,' she said; 'won't you let me ask Harry Ufford to come and spend the night? Or you could go to him. He has a room where he often puts up a friend, usually some man waiting for his divorce to come through.'

'I'd better get used to it,' Greg said. 'I'm going to get used to it. Some day I'll go upstairs again, but it won't be today or tomorrow.'

'Well, I'm a little worry-guts, I am,' said Ena. 'My old uncle used to say so. He had a 'tache like yours. I never thought I should see them become the fashion with young fellas. I wish you'd listen to me, Greg.'

'You don't imagine,' said the young man, gazing at her, 'that there'd be any danger to me? There wasn't any reason for it. It was like being struck like lightning. I'm probably safer in this house than you are in yours.'

'Well, I don't know, I'm sure,' said Ena, unhappily. 'In an old town like this there are funny old things that you forget about. It was only a year or two ago that two labourers came walking into the New Moon out of the cellars. Arthur asked them pretty sharply what they'd been doing there, and they said that they'd walked there from the High Street, from the cellar of an old house they were demolishing. Something to do with the smuggling days, everyone said.'

'You don't think,' Greg said, staring at her, 'that he got in that way? No, you're romancing, Ena. The police have been in the cellars. A fine-tooth comb wasn't in it. And they asked me if I'd unlocked the back door. So that was how he got in.'

Ena stood up and began to pile the supper-things on her tray. 'Yes, I'm sure you're right,' she said. 'I'm being silly. Funny how that story about the New Moon cellars came into my head all of a sudden. Something like this changes you, somehow. When you think of your house, normally, you think of doors and windows that lock and walls that are solid. But suddenly you find yourself thinking about windowpanes that break and bolts that don't hold and smugglers' tunnels into the cellar. Do you know, you've got your brother's eyes, exactly.'

The young man leaned back in his chair and began to laugh a little, thin chest moving under the tee-shirt with the outline of a whale. 'All right,' he said. 'You're cunning. I'm a quivering heap. Where would this Harry sleep?'

'Not "this Harry",' Ena objected. 'He'd be hurt if he thought you didn't remember him, though he'd understand why. He was a great friend of Paul's. Oh, he could sleep anywhere, the way he's lived. On this table—why not?'

'Am I a gibbering coward?' Greg wondered. 'Maybe. But I do remember Harry—yes, of course I do—and I'd like to have him about, so long as I don't have to talk to him.'

'He'll take a hint from me,' said Ena. 'When I've washed up I shall go and find him.'

'Ena,' the young man said, and put out an arm and clasped her as she reached for his cup and saucer. He nuzzled her soft plump cheek, level with his own as he sat. 'Bless you, Ena.'

'Oh, isn't he a big strong fella,' cried Ena. 'There, there. Oh, but we shall have to do something about that hair, it's only fit to wipe your boots on.'

The New Moon was probably the most ancient of the surviving Old Tornwich pubs, and had been the grandest: a rambling coaching-inn which had been overthrown in the revolution of the railway, so that in time the outbuildings of the wide yard in the shadow of the church spire had been whittled away, leaving behind half-ruinous walls of mellow red brick pressed against by self-sown elder. Internally, too, it had diminished, its clientele of fishermen and other such people in wellies imposing on it a certain surface with which they felt at home. The landlord, equally at home, changed nothing; so that, in the bars, finely worked beams fit for a gentleman's parlour looked down on a mysterious floor-covering which could once have been sodden cornflakes.

Harry came across the moonlit yard and pushed at the back door, which at first resisted, then gave with an angry judder. Men mostly in dark blue, many with knitted caps, many with beards, turned to see who he was, and he waved a casual hand to the room as he ambled on to the bar. He said to the landlord, who had his glasses on and was reading the *News of the World* with a bleak, unenjoying expression: 'Evenin, Arthur.'

The landlord put paper and glasses to one side, looking glad to be rid of them. 'Nothing but sex and murder,' he said, in a mild old-man's voice. 'You can't escape. I was sick to death of the Yorkshire Ripper from the start. I don't know why everyone who comes in here is so fascinated by people killing each other. Or themselves. Morbid lot. They come in here bursting with news: "Did you hear about old Bert, he's topped himself." Sorry, Harry. You're just the same, now I think of it.'

'Snakey old bugger you are,' Harry said, 'blackenin my character to my face. Arthur, did Frank get in? I got a message he was lookin for me.'

'Frank De Vere?' Arthur said, unenthusiastically. 'He's

in the next room, sitting by the stove, with young Dave. Guess what they're talking about.'

'I can, tonight,' Harry said. 'That puzzle my head sometimes.'

'Someone else left a message,' Arthur remembered. 'Ena came in looking for you. Said could you give her a look at the lighthouse, soon.'

'Oh-ah. Well, I don't need a pint then. I'll just find out what Frank want.'

He went up a couple of steps to the front bar, as bare and bleak as the back one, and saw Frank De Vere and a younger man seated on either side of an old iron stove, heads bent on quiet talk. In one of his almost automatic gestures of camaraderie he put a hand on Frank's shoulder, and Frank stiffened and jerked about, with a hostile look on his acne-pitted face for just a moment.

'Evening, Harry,' he said, relaxing. 'We were looking for you.'

'I heard,' Harry said, and nodded at the young man, who had a glossy black beard and a gold stud in one earlobe. 'Evenin, Dave. You're hard to find lately.'

The dark youngster looked enquiringly at Frank, who explained: 'I invited Harry to that hooley you said you were going to have, which you didn't remember to turn up for.'

'Oh,' Dave said, 'yeah. Well, sorry, Harry. I fought I'd have a house-warmin, like, but I dint get back here till late.'

'What house have *you* got to warm?' Harry wondered.

Dave was a hesitant speaker, not handy with words. 'Well, not a house, ezzackly; more a gaff, like. One of them derelict places in the High Street. You know old Fred Heaf, thass his son what inherited it, and he give me the key and said I could squat there. Thass got a reasonable roof, but I dunno—that int ideal.'

Understanding was dawning on Harry's craggy face.

'What Dave's trying to say,' explained Frank, 'is, he's shitting himself. The street door locks, but that's all that does. He thinks someone's going to shoot him while he's asleep. He's been sleeping away from Tornwich every night since last Sunday.'

'Yeh?' said Harry, neutrally.

'Frank and me fought,' Dave said, making heavy weather of it, 'that you bein a mate of the old man's—'

Harry nodded. It was not the first time that Dave's drowned fisherman father had been put to use.

'– and you havin that room where Frank was livin, and Bob, and Mick, well, p'rhaps you could put me up for a bit. I mean, that wouldn't be for long, and I'd pay you rent.'

'You would and all,' said Harry genially.

'I mean, I can't goo to Frank's because Linda—you know?'

'Depression,' Frank translated.

'So I int got a place,' Dave concluded, with relief.

Harry stood considering, fingering his lower lip.

'Well, don't just tower over us, boy,' Frank said, 'sit down and have a drink. Which Dave will bring.'

'No, thanks,' Harry said, fending off the idea with both hands. 'I've got a visit to make. Yes, all right, Dave. Just for a week or two. But I'd rather you dint come tonight. Get Frank to sleep with you, bein as you're such mates.'

The face behind the black beard looked boyishly relieved. 'You're a magic man, Harry. Fanks a lot. That don't matter about tonight. One more night there won't kill me.'

'Don't you goo jumpin to conclusions, boy,' said Harry, with a return of his normal social manner. 'Right, then: you come tomorrow with your gear about six o'clock time. I think that beard suit you. Funny what a proper black beard can do for a boy whass still wet behind the ears. Mine was always sort of gingery, for some reason.'

'Let me buy you a short, at least,' Dave said, getting up.

But Harry repelled the offer again with his tattooed hands. 'No, boy,' he said, 'no. I'm now offt, I've got a randy-voo. Frank—guard him with your life.'

Frank, still seated, had been glancing at him now and again with an expression which was probing, yet somehow wary. He had eyes of a cold, acidic blue. It annoyed Harry, that measuring look, and he returned it, and Frank picked up his beer and measured that instead.

'See you,' Harry said, in no very friendly tone, and swung round and went out through the back bar, giving the landlord a passing wave. The yard outside was bathed in fitful moonlight as black clouds were driven across the moon by a breeze which hissed and chinked over sailing-boats near at hand. The grass of the wide churchyard, and the ship-like hulk of the church with its pale-gleaming spire, whitened and dimmed by moments. A couple of the town's few trees made a chill sound. 'When winter come,' said Harry to himself, huddled inside his donkey-jacket, 'that do come.'

He left the churchyard behind him, and passed by the houses of prosperous Georgian merchants, where

44

bow-windows stared out over grass to a black sea. From behind him a ship hooted hollowly.

He made a turn, and the slim grey finger of Ena's lighthouse rose ahead, a nine-sided tower, ninety feet high, of pale brick which the sky silvered and dappled by turns. It stood in a small open place, close by where the town's main gate had been, and looked out across the water to a point where England ended.

He climbed the stairs which hugged the lower wall and banged on the heavy door. Faintly, through its thickness, he heard the King Charles spaniel begin to yap. Then Ena's voice, close, called: 'Who's there?'

His face against the jamb, he gave a bloodcurdling laugh. 'Why, gal, they call me the Tornwich Monster.' Immediately the door opened, and Ena stood there, white hair lit from behind, with disapproving black eyes under her still-black brows.

'That's the sort of silly joke we expect from you,' she said. 'But I didn't think you'd have forgotten so soon who it is who's dead.'

He was taken aback, too far to think of excusing himself. 'Just my way, Ena,' he mumbled.

'Well, come in,' she said; and he followed her into the big round room which was her living-room and also kitchen, circled by the winding stone stair which led to her bedroom and upwards. The dog immediately stopped barking and came to sniff at his shoes. The place was warm with the fuggy warmth of a paraffin heater, and shadowy with an oil-lamp and a couple of candles. 'Why the candles?' he wondered, looking about.

45

She led him towards a round table on which the lamp stood, and sat him down there by a bottle of whisky and some glasses, in the middle of the room. He looked at her from that position with a grave, apprehensive expression on his raw-boned face, making his peace after his lapse. She smiled at his contrition, and after pouring two large whiskies sat down opposite him, lifting her glass in a silent toast.

'Well, why?' he asked again. 'Thass gloomy in here.'

'Candlelight for seduction,' Ena murmured. 'Oh, because I'm a daft old woman and keep forgetting to pay my bills.'

'Ena,' he said, 'you int short, are you? I mean, you on'y got to say. With this job with Marlowes I'm earnin more than I know what to do with.'

'No, truly,' Ena said. 'I truly did just overlook it. Though I do find myself hoping, sometimes in the middle of the night, that I don't live to be an old, old lady. However, that's none of your business, Harry Ufford, thanks all the same.'

He looked at her broodingly in the lamplight, then raised his glass to her. On a hulking old-fashioned sideboard behind her, awkwardly placed against the round wall, were many photographs. Her young merchant seaman husband, torpedoed in the Atlantic. Her small son in the year of his death, with the cherry lips, cerulean eyes and butter-coloured hair of a tinted studio portrait of those days.

'I'm glad you came,' she said, 'I wanted to ask you to do something. I think someone should go and spend the night in that house with Greg.'

He was surprised, but thought about it, lowering his eyes and biting his lip as he did when he was thinking. Absently he took out his battered tobacco tin and rolled a cigarette.

'Oh, don't say you can't,' she said. 'I've as good as promised the poor boy.'

'Yes, I can,' he said. 'I shall feed my cat, then goo to him. Just the one night, bein as I've got the day off tomorrow. Oh, guess what, Ena, I'm goonna have the pleasure of Dave Stutton's company in my top room, because of all this. And I'd been hopin you might persuade Greg to come there. Would you credit it, here am I in my middle years playin babysitter to not one but two strappin young fellas of twenty-four.'

'Well, Greg is different,' said Ena. 'He's not the sort to take advantage, not like young Dave. And I wouldn't call him "strapping", either. I'd call him nervous, and not just because of this.'

'It's the brains,' Harry said. 'The brains make them high-strung.'

'I'm surprised Dave doesn't stay with Frank,' Ena said. 'They seem as thick as thieves.'

'Yeh—don't they,' said Harry, meditating.

'I don't like that Frank. I think he's creepy.'

'Have you ever been in his house?' Harry asked. 'No, of course, you wouldn't have. Well, I have, and thass what I thought: "creepy". I mean, I quite like that sort of thing myself, but thass a bit over the top. I mean, all over the walls of his front-room there's all these old guns, pistols, swords, daggers, the whole lot. About a month ago he had a social call from a young copper about something or other, and that boy was very interested. I mean, really interested, because thass an interestin collection, and I s'ppoose coppers have hobbies like other people. But he ask Frank if all the fire-arms was put out of action, like, and some weren't, and Frank got a friendly warning about that, and another visit later to check up. Well, Frank's wife—I don't think you know her, but she's kind of funny, nervy—she dint like that at all. She get all flustered about lettin a meter-reader into her house, so you can guess how much she fancied havin a policeman there, twice. Frank told me she wanted to put the whole lot out for the dustman, hundreds of quids worth. I don't think that story's over yet, so if you're in the market for something like a blunderbuss, I'll put in a word.'

'I think that all sounds rather nasty,' Ena said, 'especially if his wife's like that. But there are lots like him. Men and their toys.'

'His father was in the army,' Harry said, 'I s'ppoose that explain it. Squaddy, I think, then NCO. Frank lived quite a lot in Germany when he was a boy. He speak German. I've had nights out with him in Hamburg and Bremerhaven.'

A clock on the sideboard whirred and gave a faltering chime. 'Oh, Harry,' Ena exclaimed, 'how you do go on. It's half-past ten, and Greg thinks you're on your way. Do make a move, because he needs all his sleep.'

He was rising even as he emptied his glass, and followed her to the door, the dog trailing after. From the high step they looked out on streets quite empty, on blank windows catching the intermittent moon, on slate roofs tinged blue by the same light.

'So many empty houses,' Ena mused. 'There's only you near, and you'll be away tonight.'

'Well, Eddystone Ena,' said Harry, 'you int so badly off. I've heard tell of lighthouses what int even on a bus-route.'

'Get along with you,' Ena said, shoving between his shoulderblades. 'I'll tell you what: you and Greg come here for breakfast. Promise?'

'Okay,' Harry said. 'I'll put it to him. Night, Ena.' He went on down the steps with a hand on the chill railing, and heard the door of her tower bang shut against the breeze.

...The monster
meant to attack Heorot after the blue hour,
when black night has settled over all—
when shadowy shapes come shrithing
dark beneath the clouds.

Beowulf, tr. Kevin Crossley-Holland

Inside, beyond the small squares of dimly lit curtains, she hovers, but busily. There are two glasses to be rinsed in a basin, a bottle to be stowed away in the sideboard. There her eyes take in the photographs, but routinely, because they are household objects of every day, not often now connected with the real people who faced self-consciously into the camera.

The dog is sprawled by the blue-burning heater, but when she moves lifts its black and tan head to watch her.

She looks at a plant on a window-ledge of the round room, and tests its soil with a forefinger, and does not water it.

She returns to the table to wipe it with a yellow cloth.

On the table is a battered tin, which she picks up, clicking her tongue. She looks towards the door, as if chiding him for his forgetfulness. The tobacco-tin is old, its paint almost removed by years of lurking in pockets. She thinks how attached men grow, especially seafaring men, to trivial objects which they can carry with them.

The curving steps, layers of black and silver. The iron railing, almost icy now.

51

At the sound of a knock she stops, one imagines, in her hovering way. She looks, one imagines, at the door, alert, birdlike.

Her voice comes from close. 'Harry? Yes, it's here, your tobacco.'

The door opens on the dim light, and she is standing there, plump hand clasping the tin below her thrusting little bosom, face prepared in an expression of jocular reproof.

Her eyes have all at once a mad fixity, and reflect the moon. Her mouth begins to open on teeth all at once so obviously not her own.

At the sound the dog begins to yap. The dog makes a snarling rush as the body slumps against the door, which gives way with creaking hinges and retreats into the room. The tin rattles to the floor and spills tobacco.

Now all that she has been is opened to me.

3

TO CLOTHE A SHADOW

Indolent Linda De Vere was woken at nine, having watched a film on BBC2 until an early hour, by the coyly nagging beep of her digital alarm clock. Her husband was gone, of course; she had a recollection of having been brought half awake, an hour or two earlier, by his leaving. He had been in bed and asleep for some time when she had come upstairs, and this was becoming routine, in the second year of their marriage.

She loved her bed, he often said, less indulgently than at first. He had a theory, or had heard a theory, that people like her were the result of induced births, and was delighted when her mother, in a letter, confirmed that Linda was such a birth. She had some sort of sense of it herself, cocooned in her warm sheets, wanting not to be born. She liked to lie in the mornings, after he had gone, and watch the sky over the roof-ridges opposite, and the gulls which came dipping down into the narrow street. The gulls came even in the middle of snow, when the roofs were white and the flakes often blew upwards, like seeding willow-herb.

She could not, however, decently allow herself very much of that, and was soon in the bathroom, facing up to the fact of her birth. On the glass shelf over the basin she noticed a couple of lipsticks, and wondered at them, but decided that Frank, hunting for something else, had taken them out and forgotten them. They were darker than any she had used for some time, and she thought it would not be wasteful to throw them away. They were loud, and she was quiet and pale: pale-lipped, pale-skinned, with unre-markable blonde hair and large grey-blue eyes which looked vague, being short-sighted.

Downstairs in the kitchen she made herself a cup of coffee and took it into the sitting-room to the chair facing the television set. She liked her room, snug with central heating, though Frank's museum of firearms and bladed weapons on all the walls jarred on her now, bringing back an argument in which frayed nerves had showed. Later, cooler, she had told him that he could have a proper man's den all of his own for his murderous things, and a Hornby train too if he liked. But he always thought of that room as a nursery, and nothing had been done, and no more said.

She was often extremely nervous. In her sea-days, the boring days of a stewardess on a ferry, there had been little epiphanies of panic, when she suddenly saw all the hills and valleys below her and thought that she was, in effect, flying, and might fall. Creakings and pitchings and judderings in the middle of the night had sometimes made her heart jump. And there had been far too many people in her sort of sea-life, people against whom she could not lock her door.

She read a good deal, in that armchair, often returning to certain old volumes which were in the small bookcase. She liked novels about large houses with a history, and servants, and secrets. *Rebecca* and *Gone With The Wind* were her great favourites, and sometimes she would slip back into a more genteel century and live for a while in *Jane Eyre* or *The Woman in White* or *Uncle Silas*. Of recent books, she loved *The Thorn Birds*, and quite liked *The French Lieutenant's Woman*.

It was as she was putting down her empty cup on a table that she noticed the writing on the windowpane, a little blurred by the net-curtain. She got up, cigarette in hand, and crossed the room to examine it. She did not draw the curtain, in case some passer-by should see her and think her odd. But she made out that the writing was inside the glass, and in a lipstick which she had worn only once. It had been too bright, a mistake.

The message, in very regular capitals, read:

NOT TONIGHT:
SOON

The Os of the last word had irises and pupils.

The thought of such playfulness, if that was what it was, on the part of her husband made her tired. Listlessly, a little fretfully, as if to him, she said: 'And what the fuck is *that* supposed to mean?'

*

Commander Pryke's house, which dated from the late fifteenth century, was in strong contrast with its Georgian neighbour across the way. Paul Ramsey's tall barrack was austere, inside and out; but the Commander's interior was beamy, chintzy, rosewoody, with an occasional touch of oriental brass. Everywhere were signs of the hand of the late Mrs Pryke, whose portrait, tolerably painted, looked down from above the drawing-room fireplace. There were photographs of her, too, on piano and bookshelves, producing the composite impression of a wartime young lady with some good prewar clothes, and a patient dutiful face in the manner of Celia Johnson.

Among the photographs were some of her husband at similar ages: always in uniform and tensely self-conscious, with a lean trim neat-featured face which might in those days have been called handsome, but never interesting.

The Commander, drinking a whisky in one of the twin armchairs in front of the fire, was having some thoughts about Greg Ramsey, in the other. One didn't, he was thinking, want a young fellow to be a windbag, naturally not; but really, some of them nowadays seemed to take a pride in being almost inarticulate. It even seemed that education made them worse. The Commander rather enjoyed the company of, rather lay in wait for, a young stockbroker who came sailing at Tornwich most weekends in the summer, and at that moment found him reassuring to remember. Not much brain there, and a certain coldness of the eye which could be offputting when one noticed it; but a decent, a thoroughly civilized flow of words when they were called for. Greg Ramsey, with his abrupt utterances eked out with unilluminating, un-English gestures (like some Maltese or Malay fisherman, the Commander thought, trying to explain something), was definitely hard work and probably a sign of what universities had become.

He cleared his throat and asked: 'Drink all right?'

The boy (the Commander knew that he was twenty-four, but he had the cut of a teenager) held up his glass to show that he had hardly touched it, and said: 'Fine, thanks.'

The heavy, fashionable moustache had begun to look false on that haggard young face, above that childish mouth.

'Oh, drink up,' said the Commander, showing him how it was done. 'It could do us irreparable good.'

'Lead in your pencil,' the boy toasted, wanly smiling, 'sir.'

The Commander got up to refill his glass, and from the table murmured: 'Dreadful. Incredible. I mean, literally—incredible.'

When he looked round he saw that Greg Ramsey was sitting on the edge of his chair, chin on his chest, moving his head from side to side. His awkward blue-denimed limbs looked broken.

'I say,' said the Commander, 'Greg—'

'I didn't really know her until yesterday,' the boy said, in a boy's voice. 'Last night I gave her a hug, she was so nice. She was so nice.'

'Dreadful,' the Commander said again. A shy impulse drove him to lay a hand on the thin blue shoulder turned away from him, before taking his drink to his chair.

'You don't know what to do,' Greg said, into the fire. 'You don't know what to think. It's so—so wanton. There's no sense, no feeling, not even of hate, no motive.'

'There might be, you know,' said the Commander. 'I mean to say, it's hard to believe that a lively widow, who must have been quite attractive once, had no man at all in her life for forty years. I'm sure there is a motive to be found, however mad it may be, somewhere in her past.'

'Yes,' Greg said, with one of his unhelpful gestures. 'Oh yes. They'll be rummaging through her past now, as they're rummaging through everything she had.'

'It has to be done, my boy. Nobody does such a thing entirely without motive.'

Greg turned his head. 'And my brother?'

'Well, there, too,' said the Commander, a little flustered, 'there probably was one. Nothing discreditable to your brother, I'm sure, and I didn't mean to imply that, any more than I meant to suggest anything fishy in the background of that poor, nice little woman. But dammit, Greg, man is a motivated animal. There must be some reason, some connection that makes sense, even if only to a deranged mind.'

'Did I look offended?' Greg asked. 'Sorry. I wasn't. My mind was wandering.'

'I'll tell you what, young fella,' the Commander said, 'you'd do well to get out of that house and go back to where you came from. Even when the circumstances are normal, it's not easy to live in the middle of—another person's clutter.'

The young man shook his head, and took a token sip of his whisky. After a moment he said: 'I would always have to keep in touch, anyway. I'm a suspect, I suppose.'

'You!' exclaimed the Commander, feigning shock. 'Oh, what rot. Why, you weren't even here—the first time.'

'No,' Greg agreed. 'But I left London rather early on a Sunday morning. There might be somebody who could swear to seeing my car parked there all night; but I doubt that, in the heart of bedsitter-land. I can't think of anyone there who would know my car, or me, either.'

The Commander mused about that. 'Seems odd to me, the idea of being so totally anonymous. Of course, Conrad was right: a sailor leads the most sedentary of lives, taking his house with him like a snail. It's you bedsitter-dwellers who navigate the unknown.'

'Not me,' Greg said, 'not normally. I just borrowed this place in London for a few weeks. So sailors do read Conrad, Commander?'

'Some do,' said the Commander. 'I used to. Rather deep. Not very cheerful, but—well, that's true to life, isn't it?'

'Someone who knew him,' Greg said, 'I think it was Bertrand Russell, said he was like a man walking on a crust over molten lava, expecting at any minute to fall through. In the last eight days I've come to understand what that means. Oh God. When I saw her, I had a feeling—apart from what I was feeling for her—a feeling for myself, of dread, of absolute dread.'

'*You* saw her?' said the Commander, staring. 'I understood that Harry Ufford—'

'I was with him,' Greg said, sounding tired. 'Apparently she'd invited us there for breakfast, and Harry held me to that, although it was lateish, near nine. When the dog heard us on the steps, it started to go mad. Then we saw that the door was slightly ajar, and the dog was snarling and prancing in the opening. And then we both guessed.'

59

The Commander said, sincerely: 'I'm so sorry, Greg.'

'She was lying just inside, as she must have fallen. It was the same as before. Through the forehead, but this time point-blank.'

'Frightful,' breathed the Commander. 'Oh, foul.'

'Harry was so grim, and silent. I hardly recognized him. Until he picked up the dog, to quieten it, and then he cried a bit. That was when I felt the dread.'

'If Harry,' said the Commander, 'were to find this person before the police, he would do something terrible.'

'So would I,' said the young man. 'I would be—atrocious.'

The Commander, whose political discussions, or tantrums, often turned on the point of law and order, thought to insert a word there, but put away the idea because the boy was not really with him, but back in the two violated rooms. So instead he reached forward with the poker, and made a bigger blaze for the lad to gaze at.

'We're doing,' Greg said, 'what must be being done in nearly every other place in these streets where two or more people are together. Rummaging. Getting together rags to clothe the shadow. That's what they'll be doing. Like in that Wells story: bandaging the Invisible Man. In somebody's life there are the rags that will make the shadow take shape when it is dressed with them.'

'Not someone we know,' objected the Commander. 'Oh no, dear chap. Some stranger, some prowler from outside, that is quite obvious. With a motive or without one—if you insist—but a stranger. Don't you agree?'

The young man shrugged, and sank back into his chair

60

away from the fire's new blaze. 'Funny enough, as Harry would say, I don't think very much about it. One doesn't. One thinks of the one who's gone. I keep thinking of Paul and all he did for me, and wondering if he thought I took too much for granted. I did at one time, I know. I had rather the feeling in those days that he was too old to have a life of his own.'

The Commander leaned his head back and looked at the painted face of his wife with its reserved smile. '*Tu n'as rien à te reprocher*,' he said. 'My wife used to quote that. She had a poor sad French woman-friend with a bedridden old mother, and that was her guiding principle: that the most important thing in life was to have nothing to reproach oneself for, with respect to the dead.'

'Are there such people?' Greg asked. 'If so, they're thick, I'd guess.'

The Commander said nothing, but went on staring at the portrait, in a rapt lethargy, just as his visitor stared at the fire.

Harry was showing Dave Stutton his new quarters, in the room at the top of Harry's tall thin house. 'Thass a bit Spartan, like,' said Harry, 'but thass got what you need, I s'ppoose. Bed, cupboard, drawers. There's a foo bits of gear of mine stowed away up here, but I shan't be botherin you, I never come up this far.'

Dave, at the window, peering down, remarked: 'Thass a bit like a lighthouse here,' and then looked awkward.

But Harry seemed not to have heard, and only said, after a moment: 'Well, you get yourself settled, boy, and I'll give you a drink when you come down. No supper, though; I didn't buy no food today, what with the coppers and that. I thought I'd goo to the Galley, myself. You?'

'Yeh,' Dave said, 'sure. Fanks for everyfing, Harry.'

'You're welcome, boy,' said Harry, at the door, with a genial smile, which faded, however, even before he turned.

When Dave, later, followed him down two flights of stairs he found him sitting in his chair with the little dog in his lap. From the corner of the fireplace the cat was looking on balefully. 'Problems,' Harry said to Dave. 'I got problems. Oh you bad boy, you greeneyed monster, Rover.'

Dave pointed a finger at the toy dog. 'You call that fing Rover?'

'Rover's the cat,' Harry explained. 'I don't think I ever heard the name of the dog. Ena just useta call her silly names, like Tiddles and that.'

'Thass a good name for a dog,' Dave said. 'A good name for *that* dog. Tiddles—kill!'

'Cut that out, boy,' Harry said, as the dog started. 'She's in a state. Her nerves are shot to pieces, and my jealous old cat int helpin. Poor little old dog.' He brought his forehead down to rest for a moment against the spaniel's.

'You goonna keep 'er?' Dave asked.

'I reckon,' said Harry, gazing into the dog's face. 'Oh, if you could on'y talk. Just think of it, Dave: these bright little eyes have sin it, sin the man with the gun. This is the on'y witness there is.'

'Everyone,' Dave said, 'say: "The man", but that don't have to be a man. I mean, thass not as if there was any sex in it.'

62

'Thass what makes it all the more pecooliar,' said Harry, musing. 'I mean, this sort of thing, thass nearly always about sex. And then half the commoonity can say: "Well, thass me safe." But nobody's safe here: not you or me, not the vicar's wife or the harbour master's little daughter, not even the dogs and cats, seein he seem to be doin it just for a giggle.'

'They say thass some foreign seaman,' Dave said. 'Yugoslav, that'd be my guess.'

'Oh, what shit,' Harry muttered. '*They* say. *They* int got a clue, boy, and well you know it. And why Yugoslav, anyway?'

'I don't like 'em,' Dave admitted.

'There, you see? Thass ezzackly what I mean.'

He got up from his chair, the dog in his arms. 'Talkin of Yugoslav seamen and such,' he said, 'thass time we went to the Galley. I int eaten today, not a soddin crumb. I'm just beginnin to notice. I shall have to shut the dog in the kitchen where the cat can't eat her, then we're off.'

Outside the air was biting, and above the streetlamps a clear sky made the roofs gleam with icy moonlight. At the end of the narrow street which they were following a great white ship, blazing with yellow light, slid by. Harry looked at his watch. 'Late,' he said. 'Must be rough weather over there.'

Among the façades of secretive dwelling-houses the Galley's glowing windows made a festive interruption. The door, opening on steamy heat, rang a bell, and at the sound groups of men at the scattered tables looked up to see who had arrived. The strip-lighting was harsh, and the Galley

63

gleamed, in a dull fashion, because everything in it had to be washable. Some of its patrons had the trick of duelling by firing off, as it were, sauce-bottles at one another.

At a table towards the back of the large room sat a cluster of dark sailorly men. Harry murmured to Dave: 'Your Yugoslavs,' and Dave nodded.

'Off that Spanish ship,' he whispered, 'at King's Wharf—you know? They been around for a week or more. She's arrested for debt.'

'I know who they are,' said Harry, seating himself at an empty table. 'They're pretty famous among the gossips, such as you. From the way they look around 'em, I think they know it.'

'I fink the fuzz,' Dave said, as he sat down, 'might have been askin 'em about their movements, like.'

A man at another table, who had been looking at them over a plate of fish and chips, caught Harry's eye and said, economically: 'Harry,' with a nod of his cropped grey head. Harry slightly raised one hand, and returned: 'Charlie.' To Dave he explained: 'Charlie's our crane-driver, on the job.'

'What is it you're doin?' Dave asked. 'I fought you was on a dredger.'

'Not for a long time,' Harry said. 'No, Charlie and me are on this sea-defence job. You know, in St Felix Bay, where that work's bein done, buildin up the cliff? Well, thass us. We got a pontoon with a crane on it, upriver at Birkness, and we scoop up stones and shingle and that and bring it back here on our barge. Thass good money, boy; *you* need a job like that.'

'No experience,' Dave said sadly.

'You don't need it. Well, Charlie does, but me, I'm on'y a labourer now. I'll keep my eye open for you, if you like.'

'Yeh, well, fanks, Harry,' Dave said, without enthusiasm, stroking his black beard. 'Yeah, that sound like that'd suit me.'

'Where the hell's Billy?' Harry demanded of the air, and banging the table yelled: 'Bill-ee!'

The cropheaded crane-driver got up, carrying his cup of tea, and came over to take the chair beside him. He said: 'Billy's hitting the cooking sherry, I suspicion.' As he spoke, a tall fat man, with a long apron over blue-and-white cook's trousers, emerged from a rear door and bore down on them with a light but stately tread.

'Billy,' Harry said, 'where was you, boy? I'm starvin.'

Billy explained: 'Family reunion going on out the back. My daughter, with her kids. Her husband's at sea, and she's scared to stay at home alone.'

'She's one of several,' said the crane-driver. 'There'll be a few bolts and chains sold tomorrow.'

'So I didn't hear you come in,' Billy told Harry. 'Sorry. What's it to be?'

'Steak and chips,' Harry said, 'and bread and butter and a cuppa tea.'

'Twice,' said Dave.

'Quick as I can,' Billy promised, and went off, pausing for a moment in answer to some gesture from a Yugoslav seaman. His companions seemed to hold aloof from the exchange that followed, sitting hunched in their coats, and silent, like commuters.

65

'I see 'em looking a bit happier,' Charlie remarked, 'a week ago. They got old Arthur, in the Moon, to teach 'em to play darts.'

'Do they speak English?' Dave asked.

'One does, but not a lot. The oldest one, a bit bald in front, he's the pack-leader.'

'Charlie,' said Harry, 'would you reckon we could get young Dave here a job on our rig?'

The grizzled crane-driver looked the young man over. He had a long thin face, longitudinally grooved like driftwood. 'Possible,' he decided after a moment. 'Not soon, but people drop out and move on. What are you doing now?'

'Nuffin,' said Dave.

'Got to do what I can for him,' Harry said. 'His father was an old mate.'

'Yeah,' Dave said, morosely. 'Thass right.'

Fat Billy came back, silent-footed, and laid the table, reaching bare tattooed forearms around Harry's back. 'Those boys asked me,' he said, 'if I knew someone who'd change some pesetas for them. I don't know who would, and *I* can't. Feel sorry for them. Lousy position to be in.'

'Well, then,' Dave said, 'that lets *them* out. They int been doin no burglin.'

'What do you mean?' Harry demanded, shortly. 'There weren't no burglin done. I mean, no theft.'

'You know that?' Charlie asked, turning his wooden face.

'Yeh,' Harry said, 'I know it.' And he looked so grim that Charlie tactfully returned to his teacup.

Billy was looking out through the steamy window

66

traced with runnels of clearness. 'Hullo,' he said, 'here's trouble,' and padded away to his kitchen.

The bell tinkled, and Frank De Vere came in, drunk, and stood for a moment holding the door open, letting in frosty air, until Black Sam, following, gently moved him on and closed it. But still Frank stood, blue eyes blazing in his saturnine face, staring at Harry.

'Evenin, Frank,' said Harry, with a quizzical expression. 'Sam.'

Frank gave his muzzy head a slight shake, and muttered: 'Harry.'

'Come to join us? One of these days we're goonna eat.'

'No,' said Frank, with a wandering voice but eyes transfixed. 'No, I just—I was looking for Dave.'

'I'm here,' Dave said, twisting his chair about.

'No—ah—not Dave,' Frank said, 'I meant—it's Ken Heath I was looking for. He been in?'

'Not since he was a teenager,' Harry said, 'I should imagine. Not ezzackly Ken's class of caff, the Galley.'

'Yeah, well, erm—' Frank said. 'Right, Harry.' He wavered, then said to Black Sam: 'Let's try the Speedwell,' and as soon as the door was opened for him disappeared.

Sam said, grinning: 'You see 'em in all conditions in my trade.' He followed his fare out, and soon afterwards the glow of his tail-lights lit up the sweating window.

'Jesus wept,' said Charlie, 'what have you been doing to that man De Vere, Harry? You in the habit of beating him up, or something?'

'Search me,' Harry said. 'Made me think of my old cat when she get the idea she see ghosts. Well, he weren't quite as sober as what we are.'

'He often like that?' Charlie asked Dave. 'You know him?'

Dave, from under his black forelock, was watching Harry, who was fiddling with a fork. Dave's black eyes were brightly inquisitive but not intelligent. From the far end of the room the Yugoslavs were watching Harry too.

'No,' Dave said, 'I int never sin him so nervy, like, before. Harry—'

'What?' said Harry, looking up from the fork.

'Frank fink he know somefing, I reckon.'

'Or else,' Harry said, coolly, 'he think I might have a foo theories of my own, and he don't like the idea.'

'That was an act?' Charlie asked.

'I don't know, boy,' Harry said. 'Don't know what he thinks, don't properly know what I think, neither. All I know is, once you start suspectin, you might not be able to stop in time before you goo mad. Thass the mischief of it.' He lost interest in the fork which dropped from the tattooed fingers with a clang, and glanced impatiently towards the kitchen door. 'Ah, thank Christ, here come our chow at last.'

At his usual table by the window in the Speedwell Commander Pryke was improving his acquaintance with Taffy Hughes, who was something quite high up in the Customs, though the Commander had never gathered exactly what. He had known Taffy, after a fashion, for years, but it was only now, when he was bereaved of his usual companion, that the broad and portly Welshman sought him out. The Commander took that very kindly. There was a reminder of Paul Ramsey in the way bearded Taffy sucked at his pipe and sat meditating over a pint; but he was an older man by a generation, and the Commander, who was older still, had quickly fallen into a sort of younger-brotherly relation with him which Taffy's great solidity and a certain unwitherable boyishness in the Commander himself made natural. After testing him with certain political observations, about equally offensive to trendy Lefties and Visigoths, which only had the effect of making Taffy smoke with greater enjoyment, the Commander had come off it—that seemed to be Taffy's silent message—and subsided into the decent bewilderment about everything which was his normal state. He felt sorrow that this reassuring person meant to leave him as soon as his pipe was out.

The pipe was even then laid to cool in an ashtray, and Taffy showed signs of gathering his large body to rise.

'Nice to see,' said the Commander, 'that fellow—Black Sam, don't they call him?—wandering in here so naturally. I'd heard that some of the rumour-mongers had been trying to make him the scapegoat in this awful business.'

'I don't think,' said Taffy, 'that he wants to be here; or not in that company. He's been standing for twenty minutes saying nothing at all, holding a glass of fruit-juice for comfort.'

'My wife,' said the Commander, 'once had a Mrs Mop who said about some woman they both knew: "Yes, we're friends, but not *nice* friends." I should say that a lot of Frank De Vere's friends have made that discovery. As a matter of fact, I should have expected Sam to be busier than usual, in the circumstances. I don't think there'll be so many pedestrians tonight wending their way home to New Tornwich after Last Orders.'

'The pubs are very quiet,' Taffy observed. 'The family men are doing their duty. As this one should be,' he went on, raising himself on the arms of his chair. 'Oliver, this has been a very pleasant hour or so. We must foregather again.'

'I do hope so,' said the Commander, touched by the rare sound of his Christian name.

'Sam,' Taffy continued, on his feet, 'nice to see you with a little leisure for once.'

'Never for long,' Sam said, pausing on his way towards the door. His high-boned face with the everted African lips was grave. 'I had something to do for a friend, like. Evenin, Commander; quiet old night.'

'Indeed,' the Commander murmured, covertly studying his face. Sam, he decided, was not ill at ease, or different in his manner. What he was was unhappy.

Taffy was struggling into his coat. 'Wait for me, Sam. I see you're parked beside me. Oliver—till the next time.'

'Night, Commander,' said Sam.

'Good night,' the Commander said, to their backs making for the quayside door, and turned in his chair to look through the window. He watched them cross the road and pause beside their cars at the quay's edge, spinning out some polite exchange which Sam evidently found too long, for he hunched himself against the cold and dug his hands into the pockets of his jeans.

The oppressive sense of another body looming over him brought the Commander's attention back into the room, and he turned his head and looked up into the face of Frank De Vere, also intent on the two figures under the lights above the water. When De Vere looked back at him he saw that the man was drunk, which had the effect of making his exceedingly blue eyes look rather crazy.

The Commander said, not cordially: 'Evening, ah—Frank.'

'Snooping,' Frank said to himself.

'Snooping?' the Commander repeated. 'Who? Oh, Taffy, do you mean. Good heavens, no. He's the right sort, Taffy.'

Frank did not answer, but folded his arms and continued to stare through the window.

'Everyone's snooping,' he said after a while. 'Do you see, behind me, a rather squat-looking bloke at the bar? Scotland Yard, I believe. And our brave boys of the Press, risking their lives for us yet again. Snooping arseholes.'

The two cars backed out and drove away, and Frank went on staring at nothing.

'Are you all right?' the Commander enquired. 'You look a bit keyed up, if I may say so.'

With a sudden movement Frank dropped into Taffy's vacated chair. Putting his elbows on the table, and fixing the Commander with his crazy eyes, he said after a moment: 'Yes. Yes, I'm tensed up.'

'I suppose everybody is.'

'My wife is, that's for sure. That's why Sam was here. He brought young Donna, who I think is his girl, but maybe not, he brought her to sit with my wife this evening. Because she's in quite a state—my wife, I mean. I've told a lie and made a joke of it, but she's not quite sure, I think.'

The Commander, not being able to think of a thing to say, only gazed at him mildly.

'I've got to get him first,' Frank said, drunkenly gazing back. 'Short and sweet—snicker snack—and it's over.'

'Am I following you, I wonder?' the Commander mused. 'Are you talking about vigilantes, or something of that sort?'

'Something like that,' Frank agreed. 'I'm talking about one vigilante: me. Because he's threatened my life. Mine, or my wife's; probably both. So I shall have to get there first, wouldn't you say?'

'De Vere, old chap,' said the Commander, 'you're not making yourself terribly clear, I'm afraid. I shouldn't, myself, have any scruples at all about shooting down this man like a mad dog—that *is* what you're talking about?— but one must first know who he is.'

Frank De Vere laced his fingers over his chest, still intently searching the Commander's eyes. 'I do know,' he said. 'I know him, and I know the weapon. What do you say to that?'

'I say,' said the Commander hesitantly, 'as anyone would, I say that if you're of the same opinion in the morning, you must go to the police immediately.'

'Oh, shit,' Frank muttered. He dropped his arms from the table and got up. 'Good night, Commander. Thank you for your advice. Time I wasn't here.'

The Commander watched him cross the room unsteadily and go out by a side door. 'Fella's potty,' he remarked to himself. He picked up his glass, saw it was empty, and decided to have a last double whisky; because old dogs, he was discovering, liked their sleep.

As for myself, I walk abroad o' nights,
           And kill sick people groaning under walls:
           Sometimes I go about and poison wells...
Ithamore. One time I was an hostler at an inn,
           And in the night time secretly would I steal
           To travellers' chambers, and there cut their
           throats.

The Jew of Malta

I hear the door of the Speedwell bang, and soon afterwards he comes into my line of vision. A slight form, erect, but a little bowed in the shoulders, crossing the road with a measured tread towards the quay's edge, where he halts, under the pinkish-orange lights, and stands looking out over the water.

The water is broad, black, glossy. The tide is coming in. The two wide rivers drive, northwards and westwards, deep into the dark land, its rustling unleaved woods, its hibernating fields.

Again and again one gull comes with a leaflike fall into the light, is for a moment the ghost of a bird, then is caught back into the night.

He stands beneath the lamps, looking out, beyond their influence, to the clear black sky with frosty stars. Below and beyond him the red and white lights of a pilot launch rock a little on the swell.

He is always, now, in a ferment of memories. Other climates, other seas. A trick of light will bring back some place half a world away, and changed utterly by years, passed with no record except in his mind.

The stick on which he leans was given him by his wife when he came back to her finally, to stay forever. The gift said to him that he was old, with nothing before him but a little daily walking for his health. She suggested a dog, and he snapped at her. They found that they had never known each other well.

Now he carries the stick always; it is a reproach. He would like to explain to her that his irritations were with himself and with time. He remembers, from the long months of her helplessness after the first stroke, moments of impatience, perhaps understood by her, which he would like to cancel out, undo.

His profile is still that of the youth, more youthful than his years, who married her. A short straight nose, a chin just firm enough, a pink cheek. His profile, in the sights, is very Anglo-Saxon.

He hears nothing, will hear nothing ever. His arms fly up, his body twists. The stick clatters on to concrete as he disappears.

From below where he was standing a splash comes back. On the pilot launch, out of my line of sight, a man cries out.

4
THINGS CATCH UP

Soon it snowed: fat heavy flakes drifting past Linda De Vere's window as she lay in bed by daylight, past the window of the eyrie in Harry Ufford's house where Dave Stutton sat listening to loud music, over the high irregular roofs of the old town. On some days the north-easterly howled down the tunnels of the streets, searching out every chink in the close-packed houses. On others the sky was clear, the light was desert-sharp, the flat sea looked like grey silk, and lethal. On a night of rockets and exploding maroons two ships collided a mile offshore, and half a dozen people died within minutes of touching the water. The national newspapers instantly became friendly, and heaped praise on the pilots and lifeboatmen of the notorious town.

A few days after the death of Commander Pryke the idea was floated that all the males of Old and New Tornwich above the age of sixteen should be fingerprinted, with their consent. A solicitor and a schoolteacher worried in the *Tornwich & Stourford Packet* about civil rights, and Harry Ufford wrote the *Packet* a confusing letter arguing that the prints of all members of the professional classes ought to be in the records anyway. An edited but still puzzling version appeared in print, and he discussed it with Arthur in the deserted bar of the New Moon.

'Well, I can't make head or tail of it,' said Arthur, showing his usual distaste for the subject. 'From what I hear poor old Prykey was hit by a sniper, from somewhere near the telephone box. So what fingerprints could they have?'

'P'rhaps he was *in* the box,' Harry suggested. 'P'rhaps they found one there.'

'Well, good luck to them,' Arthur said; 'they'll need it. The owners of a lot of the prints they'll find there are in Turku and Antwerp and San Sebastian and even bloody Leningrad and Lagos now.'

'If it's not that,' Harry said, 'then they've found something in one of the other places. They int all that stoopid, Arthur. I read a lot of books about how they work in this sort of case.'

'You and all the rest of the ghouls who drink here,' said Arthur. 'Kinky, I call it.'

'Well, we int ezzackly crowded out with ghouls,' said Harry, 'are we? I mean, I can still sort of move my elbows, like, tonight.'

'You know what it is?' said Arthur. 'It's that outside Gents of mine. Nobody dares risk a pee in case he gets shot.

I'll let you use the Ladies, if you need it. Not many ladies get in here lately.'

'I int scared of your bog,' Harry said. 'Glad I int a milkman, though. They're the jumpiest boys outside Ulster these dark mornins.'

'It'll all blow over,' Arthur said. 'I'd put a tenner on that. What is it—two weeks since the Commander? Poor old boy. He was the same age as me. Well, he had no one to leave behind, and I suppose that's a sort of a mercy. How's that young brother of Paul's? I haven't seen him since they used to get in here sometimes of a weekend.'

'I've seen him better,' Harry said. 'Things catch up with you, know what I mean? It's sort of—I dunno, weird, and 'orrible—that the three what was picked out was *that* three. You'd think that whoever it is was tryin to kill Greg too, tryin to sort of kill him inside, like.'

'Three in a cluster,' Arthur said, 'then a fortnight with nothing. I think it's over, Harry. I don't think I'm going to have to bring my Gents indoors. A nine days' wonder, which will never be solved, I bet.'

Harry was looking moody. 'But that's got to be,' he said. 'We can't live with that unsolved. Christ, Arthur, you're a proper cheerer-upper, you are. Now you've got me thinkin about that lad, that young Greg. He's—' Harry said, and paused, brow ridged with searching for the right word, 'he's wiped out, like, know what I mean?'

Greg Ramsey seldom went upstairs in his brother's house, and never into the room in which his brother died. Now and again, more and more rarely, the telephone would ring in that room, behind the closed door, but he made no move to answer it. He had arrived in Tornwich the last time with most of his possessions in his car, and before long had turned the downstairs sitting-room into an average student bedsit, where he spent most of his days listening to records or playing his guitar, or lying in his sleeping-bag with a book in his hand.

The house was cold, but he did nothing about that except to switch on an electric fire. The meals he cooked for himself were usually vegetarian, and most often of baked beans. Washing-up piled in the shining new kitchen, which gradually acquired a greasy patina and a sour smell. One night, lying sleepless, he heard one of the taps dripping into the filled sink, and because he liked the sound in the empty house he set it dripping every night before he went to bed. Later he bought from a nearby antique shop a Victorian cottage clock with a loud tick and chime, and placed it in the house so that the sounds of clock and water-drip came to him at the same volume as he lay in the dark.

He had not shaved since the day of his brother's funeral, and rather slowly grew a sparse blondish beard. His clothes were washed, not very often, in the bath. After a while it became apparent that he need not leave the house except for a quarter of an hour once a week to buy food.

He was scrupulous in his attention to chains and bolts and window-catches. It was generally accepted that his brother's murderer had entered the house by the unlocked back door, which opened on a small blind yard, after climbing the high wall dividing that from the yard of an empty house. The two bolts on the back door were always shot home.

The cellar door, which opened outwards, he kept bolted at first, but later he nailed it up with two lengths of timber, and after that lay easier at nights, listening to his tap and his clock.

He became increasingly disturbed about the postman, and formed the habit of always waking before he came. It worried him that this stranger could intrude objects, could even perhaps intrude his hand or arm, out of the world into his private space. Of all threats in the house, the letterbox threatened most. But letters for his brother continued to invade, and he piled them on the dining-room table for someone to attend to some day. Often he had strange suspicions, and would stand staring at some object which he thought had been displaced by another hand. From the dining-room he could occasionally glimpse strangers moving about behind the windows of the late Commander Pryke.

He heard from Harry that the Commander's house was soon to be for sale. The visits of Harry were no distress to him, but an abiding difficulty, because he could no longer find the things to say that people said to one another. Harry wanted to take him out of himself, which meant to a pub, and he invented a recent history of hepatitis with no attempt to be credible. Harry was insistent that he should see people of his own age, and brought him as visitors Dave Stutton, who sat speechless and grinning in an agony of awkwardness, and a girl called Donna, who said things like: 'Pudden?' and 'You what?' but looked threateningly ironical and intelligent.

He took to pinning on the door notes saying HARRY—GONE WALKING IN THE COUNTRY, or

HARRY—GONE TO LONDON ON BUSINESS. The visits continued, but tailed off.

The nights when he was supposed to be away he spent lying in the dark, listening to the water-drip, the tick and the chime. Sometimes the telephone, felt as hardly more than a vibration of the ceiling, rang in the tabooed room. For two or three days in late November it rang continually.

One day he was woken by the sound he had expected and feared, heavy raps of the knocker on the door. It was not Harry, it was not the sound or the spirit of Harry. He could not tell what time it was, his watch had stopped, but he felt a conviction that he was at last to meet the postman.

He got out of his sleeping-bag, and he was naked. His hands were shaking as he pulled on clothes. Outside in the street it was snowing, but the strange car parked near his window had almost no snow on it.

In the hall he removed the chain, he slipped back two bolts, he made himself open to the stranger.

The slight woman on the snowy step was shivering inside a sheepskin coat, and beating her hands in bright folksy gloves. A headscarf made her unfamiliar. She was staring at him.

'Greg,' she cried, 'what *is* going on? Why don't you answer my letters? Are you *never* in when I ring? Greg, I'm absolutely in the dark about you.'

'Diana,' he murmured, recognizing his brother's betrayer, bent on coming in.

Diana Ramsey was a petite dark woman of thirty, with a rather diffident manner contradicted by a rather imperious

80

voice. She had always seemed, to her brother-in-law, like a schoolgirl taking on the role of hostess before she was at home with it, and therefore overacting a little: her expressions of pleasure too emphatic, her talkativeness with unpromising material like himself threatening to go over the top. But her hostessly ways served her while she examined what he had done, in a few weeks, with the fruits of her taste and planning. 'Oh dear,' was the worst she had to say of the kitchen. 'Well, all men are born bachelors.'

But the pile of mail on the dining-room table did throw her a little. 'Oh, Greg,' she sighed, skimming through the envelopes, 'how *could* you? And here are my letters to you, and some others addressed to you, too. Haven't you even looked at them?'

'No,' he said. 'I thought they were all for Paul. I thought you would come, or a solicitor, or somebody.'

'And I did come,' she said. 'Obviously I had to. I suppose you thought the telephone calls were not for you, either.'

'I never go into that room,' he said. 'I thought that the police would rather I didn't.'

At the mention of the police she looked grim for a moment. Then she said: 'Even the police, above all the police, know that life goes on.'

He said the first thing to her that had not been dragged out of him. He said: 'Is it your house, Diana?'

She looked up from the letters, sidelong. 'Do you mind that, Greg?'

'No,' he said. 'Why should I? It's usual. It's what I expected.'

'I don't want it. Truly. Will you let me give it to you?'

He made one of his vehement, inappropriate gestures, rejecting the idea. 'That would be silly.'

'No,' she said with conviction. 'Not silly at all. But we needn't talk about it just yet.'

He bowed his head, in doubting agreement.

He had hoped that she would put all the letters into her car and drive away with them to wherever it was, Pimlico he thought, that her lover had his pad or swinging studio. But she had meant all along to stay for a day or two, and now saw that she must stay for a week. There was so much to be done after a death, and it was she who must do it, the paperwork, she meant. As for the housework, well, there she would expect some help. In the kitchen, while he dried dishes for her, she made an attempt to jolly him along about his slovenly ways. 'Dear Greg,' she said, growing sentimental at one point, 'we were good friends, weren't we? Not, perhaps, just at first—you did make me feel a little bit like a stepmother at first—but later, it was fun.'

Sometimes he had the feeling that, far behind his eyes, there was another pair of eyes, watching her down two dark tunnels.

In the evening she called downstairs for him to come and join her in a drink. At the open door of the room he hesitated, feeling in his body a physical reluctance to go further. His brother's chair had been moved, and a small cushion which had been behind his head was gone. Had the police taken it? Or had she, a few minutes before, capably tidied it away, with her husband's life-blood on it?

Her remarks about his silence became less playful, and began to sound a little fretful. But he clung to it, because he knew that if he once began to talk he would never be able to stop, just as he knew that if he once began to weep he would break in two.

She slept that night in her usual place, and in the morning she asked him to come with her to the bedroom. 'This is always a dreadful moment,' she said, throwing open a wardrobe; and she asked him to choose whatever he could use from among his brother's clothes. The rest she would give to the church.

He said, with a sort of horror: 'No—no, don't.' And when she looked surprised, he said more calmly: 'Leave all his things, just leave them. There is a lot here that I could use. I mean, I haven't got much of anything. We professional students don't.'

She closed the doors in silence, then asked: 'What will you do, Greg?'

'I don't know,' he said. 'What will I do when?'

'Will you stay here? I wish you would, and yet—is it good for you?'

He did a wan imitation of Harry. 'I reckon that int bad, gal. I mean to say, thass a roof over my head.'

'Funny old Harry,' she said.

For a moment he was almost expansive. 'It was Harry who arranged the funeral. Harry and Whatshisname, the headmaster. Harry's not particularly practical himself, but he knows so many people that he can get nearly anything done.'

'I know,' she said quietly. 'Harry and I spoke on the telephone, several times. I'm sorry, Greg, but I couldn't come. For every kind of reason, I just couldn't.'

'Oh, I understood that,' he said.

'Did you? Well, that's by the way. Though it's a relief, I must tell you, to know that you weren't ignoring my letters deliberately, only accidentally. But we were talking about your living here. Isn't it very lonely?'

'No,' he said, 'no, I've lots of friends here. There's Harry, and a young guy called Dave, and a girl called Donna, and Frank De Vere, and Arthur, the landlord of the Moon, and Bob the grocer. If I can, I'd like to stay in Tornwich through the summer.'

'Of course you can,' she said. 'I suppose you're hoping for a job in the autumn?'

'Hoping,' he said.

'And there's a Donna, is there? That sounds cheerful.'

'It was Donna,' he said, 'who got me to board up the cellar door. She's a nervous girl. She's heard of these old smugglers' tunnels.'

'What nonsense,' Diana said. 'But—well, it's very satisfactory.' Passing him to go to the door she took his hand and gave it a light squeeze.

He was sure he did not hate her, but whatever it was that watched her through his eyes watched very coldly. You took him away, it was thinking; but he came back again, hurt.

If he cried, a fault-line would appear between the two tears, and he would crack apart in neat halves.

She was indulgent, exaggerating, as she always had, the difference between their ages. But she was firm. She had not designed the sitting-room on the ground floor for unemployed Ph.Ds to crash in. 'Why waste those empty rooms on the second floor?' she asked, friendly and managing.

'We'll do it together, make a proper bedroom for you. It will be fun, Greg.'

But he insisted on attending to it himself, doing no more than sweep the bare boards before lugging his possessions upstairs and dumping them in the large room. He had a colourful piece of garden furniture for sleeping on, and his record-player and his loud clock for company.

In the changed state of affairs he preferred to be up under the roof. She assumed that he went out sometimes, and he let her think so.

Over meals she was sometimes playful, in a maternal way. 'Oh, Greg,' she said, after some new proof of his impracticality, 'you are a pillock.' He guessed that the word was borrowed from her lover's vocabulary, but found it apt. He visualized a pillock as a sort of phallus made of marshmallow. He felt like a pillock.

Their meals together he found very long. When they were met over a table he discovered great faults in her. He knew that he would have found others, perhaps worse, in anybody else; but then, no other human creature had so sought him out, thrust its company upon him. At times he felt driven to tell her about her shortcomings, but knew that if once he began to speak he would never stop, that it would be the beginning of something violent and irrevocable.

She stayed for a week, and then one morning he carried her things out to the car. It was snowing again, and she was well wrapped up, and when she gave him a hug was soft and yielding like a toy. 'What a scruff you are nowadays,' she said, after kissing him. Rather hesitantly, she invited him to spend Christmas at Pimlico, but seemed relieved when he made an excuse. The excuse that came into his head was Donna, and she did not press him.

She went away, with promises to come again, to telephone. Her tyres made the only marks on the snowy road.

He went back inside and shot home the two bolts, put up the chain. Then he boarded up the cellar door.

That night he could not sleep, and wandered downstairs to the room in which he had last seen his brother. Though he rarely drank except to conform, he poured himself a large whisky.

The telephone was on the same table as the drinks. He opened the telephone book and tracked down a name with his forefinger. It was two o'clock in the morning. Carefully, he dialled a number.

The voice of the man who answered was full of sleep. Hearing silence, it was at first angry, then puzzled, then angry again. He put down the receiver.

He went and sat in his brother's chair and idly picked up a little box from the table beside it. Painted on the lid in enamel was the picture of an eighteenth-century soldier, something from his childhood, something he remembered from his mother's drawing-room, perhaps on that same small table. He lifted the lid, and just as he remembered it tinkled out *Non più andrai*.

He got up and went to the telephone and dialled. This time the man's voice was, from the start, a furious bellow. He opened the lid and held the box to the mouthpiece.

When the music had played for half a minute he stopped it. The man at the other end was still listening. He could not help giving a broken laugh.

The line clicked, and he heard the purr of lost contact.

He placed the box beside the telephone and returned to his brother's chair. He leaned back and stretched his legs, studying without expression the almost untouched whisky in the glass between his thin hands.

Just before Christmas Diana rang him to renew her invitation, tentatively, and firmly he renewed his excuse. She asked about his welfare, and the house. He was able to report reassuringly of the house, because he was going through a phase of being obsessively preoccupied with it, and sometimes got up and polished silver or brass in the middle of the endless nights.

Harry, who would still often 'give him a look', as he expressed it, asked several times from the doorstep what he meant to do for Christmas. 'I don't pay much attention to it myself, but you come to mine, boy, you'll be very welcome. Dave won't be there.' He saw that he had been right in thinking Dave most unhappy in his company, and hedged about his own movements, not letting his irritation show. Knowing now that Diana talked to Harry on the telephone he was cautious, but suggested that he might, just might, go home to his native village.

But when Harry knocked on Christmas Eve he did not deny himself. He led Harry, who had the little dog with him and was none too sober, upstairs and waited upon him with alcohol. He even toasted Harry and the dog, with a sort of diffident bonhomie which made his cheeks ache.

'No,' he said, in answer to Harry's question, 'I find plenty to do. There are all these books,' he pointed out, with one of his gestures. 'I'm working, in my fashion.'

In fact, he had read nothing for two months. He had had books in his hand and had stared at them, but the print would not go in through his eyes.

When Harry had gone, he almost thought that he might venture out where people were, might go to church. In his bare bedroom he pulled down an upper sash and let midnight bells come to him on the freezing air.

At three o'clock on Christmas morning he went downstairs to the telephone. He dialled the number which was now written on the cover of the book, and played the music-box into the mouthpiece.

By the time he closed the lid the man had hung up. The purr on the line was aggressively loud, like a defiance.

He knew when it began to be spring by the birds which came back, increasing in numbers and volume as the nights shortened. At daybreak in his stark bedroom it was the blackbirds and song thrushes he noticed first. Later came woodpigeons and collared doves, whose sound made him think himself back deep in leafy countryside, until the sounds were cut across by the squawk of a gull, the bourdon of a ship's siren. The dove-voices intrigued him, hinting at hidden gardens in the blank-faced, secretive old town.

On one of his visits Harry was wearing a buttonhole of snowdrops, and said that they were always sold in the pubs in aid of the lifeboat.

The milder weather in some way changed him. In the early morning, in the walled yard which was the only place where he could stand still under the sky, and in which a few daffodils and crocuses had appeared, he felt the sea-air on his skin, and with it a wellbeing which was animal in its lack of reason.

It brought him out of the house, that tremulous sense of health and hope. He was timid at first, and pretended to be busy and purposeful, with the idea that stray glances would not have time to light on him. But most of the few people who might have recognized him were dead or gone away, and his nondescript beard and clothes made him much like any other seaman or fisherman or labourer to be seen there.

Unimportant things pleased him unreasonably: that ragwort was flowering yellow in the crevices of old walls, that fields across the estuary were bright green with new barley, that the sea was like a polished grey stone with a sheen on it, as if reflecting a blue-green sky. Oystercatchers waded and searched, gorse was brilliant in the weak sun. The crude bright colours of man, on fishermen's dinghies and on a line of beach-huts, brought back a pleasure he had once taken in a new box of coloured pencils.

In a different place, in a bay of the estuary, a plain of sea-purslane and sea-aster carved with shining brown runnels, he watched mallard waddle and swim, and flocks of dunlin skitter away like blown white smoke over the sculpted, sky-mirroring mud.

He went further afield, to the woods fringing the estuary some miles from the town. Walking towards the shore through newly green fields, in sun just warm enough to bring out the smell of grass and sea, under planing gulls and invisible larks, he felt his sense of wellbeing as an agitation, something extreme. Celandine was budding by the field edges, and in the bare woods, among fresh leaves of dog's mercury and wood-spurge, wood anemones and primroses were showing above ground. He climbed down an earth cliff to the shore and from an uprooted tree watched on the sleepy blue water a few swans drawing to them all the sky's light.

In the woods, or in some field beyond, there was a shot, and a flock of rooks rose cawing. At first he thought nothing, found nothing to think about in such an ordinary country sound. Then something must have happened, like a shadow cast over him by the wheeling black birds. He found that he had edged into a sort of cave made by the great roots of the tree. He was trembling. He could not think how to get home again.

He forced himself to his feet. He stood exposed on the sand, between woods and water, and shouted through his cupped hands. The jittery rooks took flight once more, but nobody came.

He had a habit of shutting himself up early in his room, but that night he could not sleep. The excitement of having wandered so far, and his fright on the lonely shore, had built up a tension which turned, when he was lying in the dark, to anger. That was not altogether new, but the violence of it was new. It shook his heart: that he distinctly felt, as his memory fetched back, seemed to bombard him with, instances of injustices, slights, affronts offered to him as far back in his life as he could remember. The things he had endured with such meekness made him choke now with rage, and words burst out of him, all the bitter words that ought to have been said earlier to a world which could treat him so undutifully.

'Oh sleep,' he groaned, hugging himself. 'Oh sleep, poor boy.'

He began to feel that if he tried to lie still any longer he would suffocate, and got up and threw on some clothes. He paced up and down, making wide, angry gestures at the thoughts that came into his head. His loud clock, which was slow, started with a whirr to strike midnight.

He went downstairs and poured himself a drink, and while he drank it continued to pace and gesture and mutter. Now that he had, as he felt, called the world's bluff, he longed for a confrontation with it. He wanted a fight, even if only with words: the just, lethal words which must have been in him all the time but had never insisted on being said in the days when he was dulled by docility.

As he continued to drink the words came very fluently. Fluency had never been much prized, or even trusted, by the contemporaries among whom he had spent most of his life. Taciturnity was thought more sincere. But now he was almost awed by the sincerity, pointed by gesture, of the rebukes that poured from his lips.

Eventually he had to go to the bathroom, and while he was there studied himself in the glass. Diana, he remembered, had said he was a scruff nowadays. He rebuked her, cuttingly, for that characteristic remark, and then hunted up a pair of scissors and a comb and gave his hair and beard a trim. Afterwards he washed and combed himself with care.

In the dimness of Paul's bedroom, by the light of street-lamps, he chose clothes from the wardrobe and drawers. When he had put on a white shirt and a tie, a dark suit and sober black Oxfords, he went back to the study for another drink.

The telephone was picked up as soon as he had finished dialling, but for some moments the man did not speak. At length he said, warily as usual, 'Hullo?'

'Hullo,' Greg said. 'Did I wake you? Are you in bed?'

'No,' said the man, and sounded relieved. 'Who's that?'

'You know,' Greg said, and opened the lid of the musical box for a couple of seconds. When it was closed, he added: 'Don't you?'

The man's voice had altogether changed, and was now dead tired. 'So you talk.'

'Oh, I talk sometimes. Sometimes I want to talk. I suppose you know how it is, like when you've had a drink or two, and there just isn't anyone—you know?'

'I don't know nothing,' the man said. 'I don't know who the fuck you are, or why you ring up and play that tape or whatever that is. That don't mean nothing to me. I reckon you've had the wrong number all this time.'

'No, that's not it,' Greg said. 'It's silly, but I was wanting to talk to you. But when it came to it, I couldn't get started. Very silly, that. You didn't recognize the box, then? I thought you might remember it.'

'Listen, boy,' the man said, 'you sound harmless enough, but you don't sound very well, neither. And we had a homicidal maniac here not so long ago, and p'rhaps he didn't sail away after all. The worst you've done to me so far is give me a couple of sleepless nights. All the same, I'm startin to think I won't keep this to myself no more.'

'No, why should you?' Greg agreed. 'Only, would you

come and see me, come and talk to me? I'll give you a drink. I mean, now.'

'Oh, sure thing,' said the man. 'Like a shot. Thass me you can hear knockin on the door.'

'It's all different when I'm talking to you. It all feels so quiet. Oh, come here, please. It's only a short drive from you. It's number 11 Watergate Street, opposite Commander Pryke's.'

For a long time the other man was silent. Then he said: 'That's you—Greg?'

'You don't know me,' Greg said. 'Do you? No, you don't know me.'

'I've sin you about,' the man said, 'once or twice, but that was months ago. You haven't been there all that time, have you? On your own? Christ, boy, you must be out of your tree by now.'

'I used to be clever, in a way,' Greg said, 'about acting so that people wouldn't worry about me, and so *be* a worry, as people are, you know. Diana and Harry just thought: "Well, that's Greg, he's always been quiet and a bit spineless and always had his head in the clouds." But it wasn't true; I wasn't quiet, like they thought. It was only when I started talking to you that I got quiet.'

After a long pause the man said: 'Listen, Greg, this is all very confoosin. Like you say yourself, you and me never knoo each other, so that beats me why I'm the one you want to talk to. But I think thass not a bad idea, even at this time of night. So I shall come, boy, but not just this minute.'

'Oh, that's great,' Greg said. 'That's really great. I'll leave the front door on the latch and the lights on, and you can just walk upstairs to Paul's room, you know, and I'll probably be asleep in his chair, you know, just the way it was.'

There was an intake of breath at the other end of the line, and the man said: 'Greg, I never was inside that house in my life.'

'It's very good of you,' Greg said, seeming not to have heard him, 'because it must sound so silly. But things were going wrong. I was getting so—agitated, and so—hostile, and—spiteful. But now I'm quite quiet, and I'm going to sleep for a little while, until you come, Sam.'

He replaced the receiver, and going downstairs to the street-door, removed the chain, freed the bolts and snibbed the Yale lock open. In the room above the lighted hall he found a cushion for the back of his brother's chair, and sat down and closed his eyes.

Painter.	And is this the end?
Hieronimo.	Oh no, there is no end; the end is
	death and madness.

The Spanish Tragedy

In his sleep the thin youth has sprawled in the chair. His long legs stretch out in untidy angles towards the open door. His head droops against the cushion, mouth open in the scanty beard.

The dark figure standing a few feet within the doorway says loudly, grimly: 'Greg.'

The boy starts alert, and takes up a position sitting on the edge of the chair, hands on sharp knees, sharp elbows akimbo. He stares up into the other face, with dread at first, but soon begins to laugh.

'You thought it was someone else,' he says, 'didn't you? Oh, you did. But I'm taller and thinner, and my hair's fairer, and my beard doesn't grow the same way.'

'What do you want, Greg?' the other man asks, with no expression.

The youth makes excessive gestures of ignorance, shrugging, spreading his hands. He asks after a moment: 'Why don't you come nearer, Sam? You look scared. Are you scared?'

Sam says: 'Listen, boy, I int no kamikaze. I dint come here on my own.'

The boy looks with a sort of horror at him, and beyond him, and then jumps up, screaming in a boy's voice. 'You black fucking toe-rag,' he screams, 'you ignorant fucking jungle-bunny, that wasn't what I told you to do.' In his hand is a long shining knife from the kitchen. 'I told you to come like the other times.'

'Stay there!' Sam shouts over his shoulder, and turning back to the boy, who has kept the same distance between them, he asks angrily: 'Less get this clear, young sir. Are you accoosin me, in front of witnesses, of the murder of your brother?'

'Accusing?' the boy says. 'I'm only telling you that I know. We all know. The Commander told me what people were saying. I said to the Commander: "What disgusting racial prejudice," I said, just like a liberal. But when he was dead and I heard all the details, well, I knew. I couldn't doubt it. Of course it was you, everyone knows that.'

The black man is so utterly still that for a long time after the boy has stammered into silence there is no stir in the room. At last he asks: 'Whass the knife for, Greg?'

'The knife?' repeats the boy, vaguely. 'I don't know, really. I just got used to having it near my hand when I went to sleep.'

'It's a big old house,' Sam suggests. 'You've been lonely, I should imagine.'

'Ah, lonely,' the boy says. 'It's not good. You start to get funny ideas, do you know? You say things you don't mean. Calling you raghead and coon and so on, that wasn't me, it's not how I think, I hope you believe that, Sam. I'll tell you what it was, it was that I thought it would be nice to have an argument with you. Because it's been lonely, for years it has.'

Suddenly he claps the hand not holding the knife to his eyes. 'Oh Christ,' he gasps, 'oh Christ, it's starting.' He breaks into racking sobs, and the black man leaps at him, snatching the knife, throwing it away. But at that the boy begins to flail and scream, screaming: 'Not like that, not with the knife!' as they clinch and fall to the carpet.

Other figures bound into the lighted room from the darkened landing. But there can be no more doubt in their minds than there is in the black man's that the howling, kicking child restrained in his arms is a mad child now for ever.

5
CRACKS

Harry said: 'It's like them cases you read about in the paper: like some little old cottage in a village that people walk past every day, and that look just the same as thass always looked, and nobody give it a thought. And then one day someone call, a meter-reader p'rhaps, and it come out that old Mrs Thing has been dead for a month, and everybody's amazed. I tell you what, Arthur, I'm amazed. I dint see a thing. I say to myself, I say: Well, these stoodent types, they're essentric, they're happy just playin their guitars and readin books. It was just like that cottage I was talkin about, and me gooin past and givin a wave to the window every now and then, while someone inside was dyin and wouldn't tell me.'

'You can't be blamed, Harry,' Arthur said. 'If his sister-in-law stayed there with him and didn't notice anything, no one's going to say that you should have seen more.'

'She weren't to blame, neither,' Harry said, moodily. 'Poor girl was kept in the dark, like. We know that now. Paul was that close, he never let on to her that he was worried about his little brother. Funny, innit, how we say "cracked" without thinkin what the word mean? You see, when Greg was a schoolboy he start foolin around with this what they call "acid", and have what they call a "bad crossin" or something like that, and his mind was cracked, like, and in the end that just brook along the crack. And Diana never knoo, o'ny now it come out, when thass too late to do anything. Now she find that a couple of Paul's friends knoo about it from him a long time agoo. But they dint know Greg, and anyway they thought that was a thing of the past and all cleared up now. Well, that weren't.'

Arthur said: 'Will he always be like that?'

'Dunno,' Harry said. 'I mean, the experts, they don't seem to know. What I gather, Greg int with us, properly speakin, now. Diana think he might stay like that. These friends of Paul's, they've told her that what used to worry Paul was there was something like that in their mother's family, before this "acid" was even invented. But he must have thought the danger had passed, like, before he even met Diana, prob'bly, and she never heard a word about it. Well, you wouldn't, would you, if you was courtin, tell the girl that your great-aunt Mabel finished up in a rubber room and your brother might be goonna follow.'

'You were there,' Arthur said. 'How did that come about?'

'Black Sam come and got me,' Harry said. 'Me and Dave, he asked us both to come. And then Frank De Vere, he was drivin Donna home and he see Sam's taxi outside my place, so he stop, and it end up with us all gooin. Christ, I wish we'd of kept Donna out of it. I dunno how much there is between her and Sam, but there's something, and that weren't nice, I can tell you, to be standin beside her while her fella was gettin all them, like, bigoted insults from Greg, and bein called a murderer as well. That wouldn't have been a pretty scene, anyway, but with her takin it all in that was that much worse.'

In the other bar a fisherman began to sing, to the tune of 'Land of My Fathers':

'Whales! Whales!
They're bloody great fish in the sea...'

Harry, cheering up, leaned towards the doorframe and bawled: 'Hey, Beaky, you ought to sing solo. So-low we can't fuckin hear you.'

The fisherman concluded: 'And they come to the surface to pee.'

'Things are getting back to normal,' Arthur remarked. 'We even see some ladies now, and the gents have got brave enough to use the Gents again. Somehow everyone seems to have decided the shooting's stopped.'

'I know why that is,' Harry said, gloomy once more. 'The ones what weren't already sure in their minds it was some foreign seaman have pinned it on to Greg now.'

'You can't blame them,' said Arthur. 'Well, *I* can't, because it's what I've been thinking myself.'

'Then you're wrong,' Harry said angrily. 'Sorry, Arthur, didn't mean to snap at you. But talk sense, boy.

101

You're not thinkin who that was what got killed. You can't believe he'd hurt *them*—them three particular people—or anyone else, for that matter. That poor sad kid, his trouble was he was just too harmless to survive in this world. And he int survived, poor little sod.'

'Yes, but Harry,' Arthur reasoned, 'he's out of his mind. You can't argue like that in a case like this.'

'I know a lot of people want to believe it,' Harry said. 'I'm pretty sure, and so is Diana, the police want to believe it. P'rhaps he'll end up believin it himself, and forget about Black Sam. But I int goonna believe it: I just know that int *in* the boy.'

'Why Sam?' Arthur wondered. 'Why him rather than me, for instance, or you?'

'That might be my fault,' Harry said. 'When this thing started, people were whisperin in corners that it could be Sam, among others. You must have heard that. Well, I reckon this rumour got round to Greg and stuck in his mind. I don't remember ever sayin anything about it to him, but—oh Jesus, Arthur, I think I must have.'

'I don't believe it,' Arthur said. 'Not to him, Paul's brother. Nobody would.'

'I dunno,' Harry said. 'A lot of times people just talk without thinkin who they're talkin to. Believe me, I know. Some nights I sit up and I think about them people—my friends—and the tears come into my eyes, I int ashamed to tell you. And then young Dave will come hoom with a foo beers in him and want to tell me some joke that I s'ppoose would crease me if I weren't twice his age, and my hand fair itch to smack him. Thass three months nor more now he's

102

been livin at mine, and he show no sign of movin on. Well, thass all right, I s'ppoose—on'y I never felt I understood that boy since he got to be about fourteen. Sometimes he get my rag out, talkin about Greg. Thass all "I told you so" with Dave. I took him with me once when I give Greg a look, and now he tell me he knoo all along what was up. "*I* could see he was a head-banger," he say; "why couldn't you?" I mean, that don't seem natural, when they're the same age. There ought to be more fellow-feelin.'

'I think,' said the old man, 'that's something that's in most people, but in a few it just isn't. A kind of imagination that's lacking. He might be better off without it. In the war, I came to the conclusion I had too much of it, myself.'

'Not natural not to have it,' Harry insisted. 'No man is an island.'

'You know that,' Arthur said, 'do you?'

'I think thass the name of a paperback I had,' Harry explained.

'There's more of it,' Arthur said, trying to remember. 'It goes on something like this: But each man is a part of the continent, like a promontory; and if a clod of it is washed away, the whole world is the less.'

Harry was looking at him wide-eyed. 'Is that it? Thass deep, boy.'

'In the war,' Arthur said, 'a lot of people like padres were very fond of quoting that, and there were reasons for it to stick in my mind. "Every man's death diminishes me"—that I can quote you.'

'Thass very strange,' Harry said, 'very strange that you tell that to me. I mean, here am I, spendin my days buildin

103

up this sea-defence thing, to keep the clods from fallin off the promontory. And feelin the way I do about Paul and—oh Christ, poor little Ena. And you sayin that, that bring the two things together. And thass how it feels, just like that. Like clods was fallin off me, and I was gettin smaller.'

'It tolls for thee,' said Arthur quietly.

'Howzat?' Harry asked. 'Does what for me?'

'Therefore send not,' Arthur explained, 'to know for whom the bell tolls.'

'Oh yeah,' Harry said. 'Crackin film.' He looked at his watch, and scowled. 'Shit, I've missed that one on the box, one of those about this good guy gooin around New York murderin all the bad guys. I like that kind of thing.'

In the late light the harbour was all of one colour: dove-grey. The bare woods of the far shore could hardly be separated from the smooth water and heavy sky which they divided. All the remaining light of the day seemed to be drawn to the white paint of a small freighter moving down the estuary to the sea.

Black Sam had got out of his taxi and was pacing up and down at the edge of the quay. His hands were deep in the pockets of a sheepskin coat and his body was tightened against the chill. He stopped to stare at the ship.

A tough-looking small boy in an anorak wandered past him, muttering: 'How do, Sam.' At the sound of his name the black man came down to earth suddenly, and returned: 'How do,' but with a look at the child that failed to recognize him.

The boy, pausing, identified himself. 'Killer,' he said.

104

'Oh, sure. You keepin well, Killer. D'you know that flag, Killer? I bet you know them all.'

'Thass Panama,' Killer said. 'You see a foo of them go by here.'

'Long way from home,' Sam said, absently, following the passing of the ship.

'Home?' Killer said. 'Dunno where her home would be, but not Panama. Panama's what they call a convenience. You ever been there, Sam?'

'Been where?' Sam asked. 'Oh, Panama. Christ, no; I int never been out of England.'

'Uh?' said the boy, looking disbelieving. 'I thought you come from somewhere near Panama.'

'I come from Ipswich, boy,' Sam said. 'Born and bred there. I int travelled a lot in my life.'

The boy seemed disappointed, but stuck to the subject of geography. 'My dad says thass ever so hot, like so hot it's steamy. You can see jungle, and big birds, storks or something like that. Thass a big thing, that Canal. My dad says the first time he went through there that give him quite a proud feelin about the hooman race.'

'Your dad's deep-sea,' Sam reasoned. 'Oh, I've got you. Your grandad's big Billy what has the Galley, right?'

'Thass right,' Killer said. 'You know, Sam, that surprise me that you int never been to them warm countries. I mean, I stand here watchin the ships go by, and I dream about them places, and I'm English.'

'So am I, boy,' said Sam, low.

'I mean, I s'pose you've got relations you could go and stay with.'

105

'Not a lot,' Sam muttered. Turning away from the water, he gave the child a bleak glance. 'I imagine you'll see more of faraway places than I ever shall, Killer. Well, I'm off—see you around, I expect.'

But when he had closed himself into his taxi he sat for a while, hands on the steering wheel and chin on his hands, watching the white ship glide by the grey woods and fields, on its way, presumably, to colour and the sun.

He had always been one to let things pass, in the faith that difficulties and unpleasantness could be outlived. His mother, when she was in the mood to approve, had praised him for his good cheer. His father had sometimes wondered aloud whether he understood anything at all that was going on.

He did seem to live in a world which was simpler than other people's. It was a very limited world: until he was fifteen it had consisted of a tiny house in a red-brick terrace in an arid-looking part of Ipswich, a couple of schools of similar appearance, a gentle bowery countryside for cycling and angling, and the front at Felixstowe to import, now and again, a touch of carnival. Everything had seemed predictable, and he had liked that, the ordinariness of his routines.

He had been born late and perhaps surprisingly in his mother's life, and in the small red house was an only child. Three siblings, much older, had remained in the West Indies to be raised by relations when the parents emigrated and had not chosen to follow. His two sisters he had never seen; some visits from his brother, by that time a grown man, had not been a success. His brother had quickly found some friends of whom their father passionately disapproved, though to Sam, at about five, they had seemed glamorous and amusing. It was puzzling to him, but delightful, when they produced Bibles and declaimed passages at one another, with a curious manner in which gravity was mixed up with fooling. He could remember his brother's arm around him while he intoned: 'Behold how good and how pleasant it is for brethren to dwell together in unity!' One of the friends, a jolly but very ugly youth, was fond of reciting: 'I am black, but comely,' which he pronounced 'coamly'. It was from them that Sam first heard the name 'Ras Tafari', and he had quickly learned not to repeat it in front of his parents.

His father was a labourer, his mother a cleaner at a hospital. A more conformist working-class couple than the Boskums could hardly have been found in England. Over the gas-fire in their front room hung a picture of the Queen. They would have liked the Queen to be Prime Minister also. In religion they were faithful Baptists: English Baptists. In their little rented house they lived out the narrow, private, decent lives of the Victorian artisans for whom it had been designed.

When Sam was about eleven a teacher called Miss Buxhall began to take an interest in him. This had puzzled him for a time, as at school he was good at nothing in particular, without being so bad at anything as to attract attention. Miss Buxhall, personally, left him with no strong impressions of herself, except that she seemed a sad old lady (she was in her forties, and single) and must watch television or read newspapers a great deal. By degrees he came to realize that she imagined him to be full of memories of some extraordinarily warm, extraordinarily colourful world: memories summed up in the print which she gave

107

him of a painting by someone she called 'The Douanier', all weird trees and fantastic flowers with a glimpse here and there of black bodies, and in which she wanted to have a share. The picture did, in fact, stir something like a recollection in him, but as he had never set eyes on any such scene he supposed, and told Miss Buxhall, that he must have been remembering things described to him, when he was very young, by his parents or (this interested her) his Rastafarian brother, nowadays in Kingston.

This conversation, and the picture hung beside his bed, led somehow to contact being established between the teacher and the hospital cleaner, and to a Sunday visit by Miss Buxhall to 10 Omdurman Terrace. It was a trying experience for the boy. Miss Buxhall, normal and dull enough in her own chalky habitat, seemed downright eccentric in his. She talked a good deal of the Third World, of which Mr and Mrs Boskum, though they prayed in a general way for all in need or distress, had only the vaguest notions. She spoke of the great charge of energy which was coming into the arts from the newer lands, mentioning in particular a Barbadian poet whom she had actually met after his reading ('electrifying' was her adjective) of a long poem about his African roots. Mr and Mrs Boskum betrayed a little surprise at hearing such talk in their own front room, and Mr Boskum said rather gruffly that he had never heard of the poet but knew a man of the same name who was on the railways and came from St Lucia.

If Miss Buxhall did not, in Sam's eyes, show to advantage, neither did his parents. He had never heard his mother, usually economical with her words, speak so much as she did then, in her hospitality or nervousness. And it was quite clear to him that Miss Buxhall was enjoying his mother's flow of language with the enjoyment of a keen tourist, that she found his mother *quaint*. He respected his normally garrulous father the more because he chose on that occasion to be reserved.

After that their acquaintance with Miss Buxhall trailed away into civilities, and before long he left her to go to another school. But she had had her effect. His friends had always been white boys; he had always spoken like them, and thought like them, living his life in the midst of theirs. But after Miss Buxhall, he applied himself to ironing out any slight difference which might survive. He did not mean to be *quaint*.

Nothing about him was very noticeable: he was of middling intelligence, of middling abilities in football and cricket, presentable but middling in his looks. He was popular, in a middling way, largely because of a vein of the dry humour which goes with the Suffolk voice, and because there was nothing in him to object to. He made sure that there was not. Disharmony distressed him; he was the peacemaker among his peers.

At fifteen he left school and began work in labouring jobs. For what seemed a very long time he felt disoriented in the company in which he found himself, and rather clung to old schoolmates who clearly did not think as seriously as he did about their bond. But contentment returned when he was old enough to drive. He was not the sort of youth to delight in speed and noise and random journeys into the unknown. Instead, what delighted him was the orderliness of traffic, its civilized manoeuvres and conventions. On the roads, as in the rest of his life, he was an expert dodger of collisions.

He felt that, to be happy, he had to make the roads his life, and after some time spent on the buses achieved his ambition of becoming a taxi-driver. His father died. His mother began to talk of her native island, and of the warmth and comfort her old bones might find there, in the bosom of her large and mainly female clan. They sold the little terrace house, which by then belonged to them. One day he drove her to London Airport, and returned that night to an insufficient little flat which he had had trouble in finding, and for which he had to pay too much.

He was lonely after that. What he liked best in his work was the long runs, on which a passenger might share a little of his life with him, perhaps even ask for advice. Sam was good with advice: always very safe and comforting advice which left people feeling better.

One evening, after delivering a fare to the train ferry at Old Tornwich, he wandered into the Speedwell for a beer. It was in high summer, and still light, and the view from the window over the broad blue estuary was calm as sleep.

It was then that he met Ken Heath. The boy capitalist, flushed and already slightly bloated with drink, was unbuttoned enough to want to know more about the black man with the Suffolk voice. So Sam told him the simple story of his life, and the tycoonlet exclaimed and pressed his card upon him. He was himself, he revealed, the owner of a taxi firm in New Tornwich; if Sam should ever be interested, there was money to be made. He was touchingly friendly, and Sam, who was no drinker, was taken by surprise several times on the winding estuary road.

A few days later he got out the card and rang Ken Heath. Ken sounded surprised, and a little doubtful, at hearing from him, but took his name and a telephone number at which he could be reached. Several weeks passed before he did ring, but then it was with an offer. He needed, urgently, a man to live in the flat above the taxi office. He had formed glowing opinions of Sam's reliability, and knew that he was a single man, which was what was needed, because of the telephone at all hours, and because the flat was, frankly, more of a pad.

'There's just one thing,' he said. 'I dunno quite how to put this. I don't think there's another—ah—black face, if you don't mind me mentioning it, in this town.'

'Thass fine,' Sam said. 'No problem, boy.'

A week later he was again on the estuary road, with all his possessions on the seat and in the boot behind him.

The cafe next to the taxi office was a haunt of jobless school-leavers, whose blue shapes he could see through the steamy glass as they played their electronic games, while the blare of their jukebox choices escaped into the open air, apparently through the extractor fan, and reached him as he parked. The warm office was also a favourite spot for hanging about, and when he went in he found two of them sitting on kitchen chairs watching a portable television set on the desk. The driver behind the desk had turned it away from himself and was talking to the boss, who paced and turned in the bare little room.

111

'Ah, Sam,' he said. 'Hoped I'd see you. You well?'

'A man who doesn't drink,' Sam said, 'is always well. Did you want something with me, Ken?'

'Nothing special,' Ken Heath said. 'Just to compare notes, you know. Bugger it, you can't hear yourself speak in here. How is it all the teenagers today are deaf?'

'So would you be,' Sam said, 'after ten minutes in the caff next door. Well, d'you want to come upstairs, or d'you want to go to the pub? Upstairs, you get a choice of Nescaff or Ribena.'

'That'll do,' said Ken Heath, abstracted, and as Sam held open a door for him he began rather ponderously to make his way up.

The little sitting-room above had the look of a hospital, it was so white and uncluttered. The only colour was in a large print, not a very good one, of Constable's painting of boys angling in the Stour at Stratford St Mary. The one small window had a view, by daylight, of the same river at its widest, sometimes blue, sometimes billowing like storm-tossed mushroom soup.

'You don't sound very fit, boy,' Sam remarked, as he joined his landlord. 'Out of puff after eleven stairs.'

Ken Heath's father, a jobbing builder, had bought up a number of half-ruinous Old Tornwich houses when much of the place was half-ruinous, paying almost nothing for them. Therefore his heir, in his thirties, was running to fat.

'I'm going to diet,' he said. 'Go to one of these health farms. They charge like wounded buffalo for starving you, but the sort of people who go don't mind. Conspicuous non-consumption, Taffy Hughes calls that.'

'Have a black coffee,' Sam offered.

'Shall I?' Ken wondered. 'No, I won't, thanks. You're a very tidy bloke, aren't you, Sam?'

'Drummed into me,' Sam said. 'My old mother was like that.'

'They looked the place over, didn't they? The law, I mean.'

'Yeh,' Sam said shortly.

'That can't have been very nice.'

Sam shrugged. 'I'm a law-abidin citizen. I don't want killers runnin around loose. So I don't complain.'

'Did you get any idea of what they were looking for?'

'The gun, I suppose. But they didn't tell me nothing.'

'Did they go anywhere else?'

'You're as likely to know that as what I am,' Sam pointed out. 'I heard they paid a call on Frank De Vere, because they know he's a firearms nut. That's as much as I can tell you.'

'Why you, though?' Ken Heath asked. 'You're not a firearms nut.'

'I should think,' Sam said, 'because I was on the spot just before the Commander bought it. Plus, I keep funny hours. Plus, you can't see me in the dark.'

'Ah, Sam,' said Ken Heath, uneasily. 'Lots of people keep funny hours in this town. Which is why you do.'

'All that was months ago, Ken. So why are we talkin about it tonight?'

'It's awkward,' Ken muttered, beginning to pace. 'Bloody awkward. In a way, it's none of my business—but in a way, it is. I mean, we've got competitors. If people

113

start phoning them because they're scared of one of our drivers—well, that much is my business.'

Sam was staring at him, out of a still face. 'People are scared of *me?*'

'I've got to admit,' Ken said, 'that a bit of talk has come my way. It's started again, because of that boy Ramsey.'

'That boy is mad,' Sam burst out. 'For Christ's sake, he's in an institootion. Why should it be me? Why not him?'

'Well,' Ken said, 'of course that's the first thing that came into everybody's head. But if the law have looked into it—and we know they have, and then some—and if they still don't say they've solved it, well, we can be pretty sure it wasn't that lad. So people start wondering: What if he *knew* something?'

After a moment, Sam said quietly: 'Less get this straight, Ken. People are talkin about what he said? They know about the phone calls? They know what he said to me?'

'There were several listening,' Ken said, 'and these things get out and get about.'

'Oh Christ,' Sam muttered. 'And I took them there myself. I asked them to protect me—the sneaking bastards.'

'Well, that's human nature,' Ken Heath explained. 'People talk to each other.'

Sam was standing stock-still in the middle of the room with a hand up to his forehead. Abruptly he dropped his arm and turned to face the young capitalist. 'Well, Ken?'

'Well, what?'

'What you're wanting is to break up our little partnership, I should imagine.'

'Sam, you don't understand me,' Ken Heath protested.

'You do not understand. I was *preparing* you, that's all. If this doesn't die down soon, perhaps you should spend more time in the office. At night, I mean—only at night.'

'God knows,' Sam said, 'how many local drunks I've helped through their own front doors. I've even put some of 'em to bed. This is the thanks I get: they tell each other I want to murder them.'

'It'll blow over, Sam,' soothed Ken Heath.

'Listen,' Sam said, 'tell me something. When I come in, was you talkin to Pete about this?'

'Well, yes, I touched on it, as a matter of fact.'

'In front of them two lads.'

'They couldn't have heard,' Ken said defensively. 'They were listening to the telly.'

'They were listenin to you,' Sam said. 'What have you done, boy? That int never goonna blow over now—never.'

'Shit,' said Ken to himself, and took to pacing again.

'I don't think,' Sam said, 'there's no use in talkin on about it. We better sleep on it, and think over what we've said already. You've done me a foo good turns, Ken. I shan't make your affairs more complicated than what they are.'

The fat young man paused in front of him and looked him in the eyes. 'The good turns haven't all been on one side,' he said. 'Don't get any wrong ideas, Sam—we're not parting from you.'

'Funny,' Sam said, 'that telephone's got a lot to answer for. Remember? I asked you if I could put my own name into the book with that number. On'y time I ever sin my name in print, until the inquests. That crazy fella might have never tracked me down if it hadn't been for that, and he might have just forgot about me. But that seemed sort of homely, like, and settled, bein in the phone book.'

'Time I wasn't here,' Ken Heath said.

'Time you wasn't,' Sam agreed. 'Like I said, sleep on it.'

'And you,' Ken said. At the door he made a V-sign, then went heavily down the stairs.

Sam stood staring for a moment at the picture of the angling boys, dwarfed and at home in their leafy landscape. He was wondering what had become of them all, the school-pals with whom he had gone fishing.

In the bedroom he still preserved Miss Buxhall's picture, her tropical fantasy. On the bedside table lay a neat packet of letters from his mother. It was hard to associate her with those foreign-looking stamps. She had lately passed into her seventies, and grown rather queru-lous, finding fault, in a Christian way, with daughters and grandchildren. The climate did not suit her. She dreamed sometimes of grey rainy days, of snow.

He threw himself down on the smooth counterpane, faultlessly washed and ironed. He lay staring at the spotless ceiling, painted by himself.

Listless Linda De Vere, blondely and anæmically pretty, turned down the sound of the telly so as to hear her defi-nitely blonde friend. Definite was what Donna had always been, crisp and clear-coloured. Often she gave Linda, who was the elder by eight years, the feeling of being a little bossily jollied along and mothered.

'Sorry,' she said. 'What was that?'

'I was just thinking,' Donna said, 'that it looks bigger,

the room looks bigger. Lighter, too, without all old Dick Turpin's ironmongery.'

'He flogged it all,' Linda said. 'I've told you, haven't I? He was getting the feeling that our friendly neighbourhood bobbies thought he might be kinky about shooting holes in people. Very sarky he was, about how nobody had been shot with a blunderbuss or a rapier or anything else he had. Anyway, he sold the lot, and did well out of it. I think he's good at selling things, my man.'

'I reckon,' said Donna coolly.

'Except himself,' said Frank De Vere's wife, 'as your tone is telling me. In the days when I went into pubs with him it used to get me down, the feeling of being half of an unloved couple.'

'Sometimes,' Donna said, 'you make him sound pretty unloved by you.'

'That's life,' Linda said. 'You'll find out. You fall into a rut—the sort of rut you call a relationship—and the easiest thing, on the whole, seems to be to stay in it.'

'Or the laziest thing,' said Donna.

'Christ,' Linda said, 'has he been coaching you in his lines? Give us another one. Tell me you were raised by an army wife, and you can't stand slatterns.'

'"Slattern",' Donna repeated. 'The cheeky bugger.'

'Oh, there's plenty more like that,' Linda said. 'He knows lots of words. Why did he marry me, I wonder. There must have been a female sergeant-major or two in Colchester who'd have had him.'

'Really?' said Donna, feigning belief. 'Is he that way? You know—masterful women in uniform, and all that? Whips and bondage?'

'No,' Linda said. 'No, it's the other way about. He'd like to be masterful himself, but not in a physical way. A sort of mental bullying, that's his bag. Hence the great buddyship with Dave Stutton, who's as bullyable as—'

'Two short planks,' Donna suggested.

'Right on,' said Linda.

Donna giggled a little, thinking about it. 'All the same,' she said, 'it's not really fair to him—to Frank—to talk about him like this. I mean, he was really worried about you, in the weeks after the murders. He offered to pay me—to *pay* me, for God's sake—to come and sit with you when he was out at night. I mean, he wasn't just edgy, he was neurotic.'

Linda took up a packet of cigarettes and made a slow business of removing one and lighting it. 'I suppose,' she said at last, 'he didn't tell you why?'

'Why?' Donna repeated. 'He didn't need to. There was someone going around blowing people away, that was why.'

'There was more to it,' Linda said. 'He didn't tell you anything else? About a window, for instance?'

'No. No windows came into it.'

'I was almost certain of that,' Linda said. 'Well, the reason for all the worry about me was that one morning— the morning after poor old Ena died, but before I knew about it—there was a message written in my lipstick on the inside of that window there. It seemed to be a message from the murderer, saying that he was going to call again.'

'You're kidding,' Donna breathed. 'Oh my Christ, Linda.'

'*I*'m not kidding,' Linda said. 'I've always suspected that someone else was.'

118

'You mean, Frank?'

'That was what I thought as soon as I saw it. And in spite of all his carrying on later, I never really stopped thinking that. In spite of the fact that in the end he actually *said* that he wrote it; because he wasn't even trying to be convincing. You can imagine the scene. I'd gone to bed leaving the back door unlocked—it opens on a blind yard with ten-foot walls, but so did Paul Ramsey's—and the master of the house comes down in the morning and throws a wobbler. So he grabs a lipstick which is near his razor in the bathroom cupboard, and decides he'll teach the slattern a lesson she'll never forget. That's how I read it, and if I'm unjust to him—well, I always was a mean-minded bitch.'

Donna had been staring at her, blue-eyed. 'I'm scared for you,' she said. 'Whichever way it is, whether it was him or—I'm scared for you, Linda.'

'Don't be,' Linda said. 'It was a sort of joke. The actual message was jokey. Most of his jokes have a nasty streak. People like that don't go in for physical violence, they work it out of their systems in words.'

'Deep,' said Donna. 'All the same, I don't like leaving you. But Sam will be coming for me soon. Shall I send him away again?'

'Don't you dare,' Linda said. 'Poor old Sam, faithful as—two short planks.'

'You are rotten.'

'Look, love, I've explained to you that my husband doesn't shoot people, and why. So we won't worry about that. Let's talk about something else. Let's talk about Sam.'

119

'Sam's very nice,' Donna said. 'He's sweet through and through. And he's not "poor old Sam", either. I think he's younger than you are.'

'He looks older,' Linda considered. 'Than a white man of that age, I mean. They do, don't they?'

'I hadn't noticed,' said Donna.

'Why doesn't he live with you?'

'He wasn't invited,' Donna said. 'I didn't think we were ready for that.'

'Such caution,' Linda said, 'at your time of life. Oh, tell me, sister-woman, is it true about black men? I long to know.'

'I wouldn't have a clue,' said Donna, shortly.

'You mean you've never—?'

'No. We've never.'

'You take my breath away,' Linda said. 'You must be a throwback. They haven't made girls like you since Elvis was a boy. Not even a feel of a suspender?'

'I can't explain,' Linda said, 'but it's for his sake that I've left it like this. And that was him tooting then, wasn't it? I'd better go now, if there's no point in staying.'

'There isn't,' Linda said. 'So you and I are pretty much in the same boat, gal, sex-wise.'

'True?' Donna said. 'Oh, the messes people get themselves into.'

'Why don't we run away together?' suggested Linda. 'Let's go into a nunnery. I'm sure Dave Stutton would be happy to take over my household duties.'

'Lock the back door,' Donna said. 'I think I'll go and do it now, for my own peace of mind.'

'Piss off, sister,' said her friend. 'Don't keep that nice fella waiting for everything.'

In the warm taxi parked in front of Donna's little house, Sam said: 'You're quiet. Something on your mind?'

'Yes,' Donna said. 'It weighs a ton.'

'Gonna tell me?'

'I don't think I can. No, I definitely can't. Not yet. It's just talk. We all saw with Greg Ramsey what careless talk can do.'

'You've heard,' Sam said, grim-faced, 'some talk about me?'

'About you?' Donna said. 'No, of course I haven't. Who would be talking about you?'

'You mentioned Greg Ramsey.'

'Oh, that,' said Donna, uncomfortably.

He laid his arm along the back of the seat and leaned against the door, watching her pale profile looking straight ahead. 'Tell me about that. Tell me what you thought.'

'I thought it was horrible,' she said. 'And horribly sad.'

'And him calling me a jungle-bunny and that, and a killer—what did you think of that?'

'Honestly, Sam,' Donna said, 'I didn't really listen to what he said. It wasn't his words I noticed, it was everything else about him.'

'How did you think I coped with it?' Sam persisted. 'Did you think I was dignified? Did you think I handled myself like a man?'

'You were very good,' Donna said. 'Very dignified.'

'You didn't wonder, did you, if p'rhaps he knoo something about me, something about the murders?'

She jerked her head and stared at him, her lips apart. 'Sam?'

'Did you? Did you, Donna?'

'I'm going indoors,' she said, groping for the door-handle. 'You're scaring me. If it's a joke, it's not like one of yours.'

'No, no, no,' he soothed, touching her neck with his fingertips. 'I'm sorry, little gal, I rushed into that clumsy, like. What I meant was, someone who was there has been talkin about it, and suspectin Greg Ramsey knoo something the coppers don't know.'

'Oh, I see,' said Donna, relaxing a little. 'That bloody Dave. Well, it might have been Frank, but I bet it was Dave—that hairy wally.'

'I don't need to repeat my question,' Sam said. 'Just for a moment you was terrified. You thought you was sittin in a dark car with a murderer.'

'Oh, don't go on, Sam,' Donna begged. 'I'm very jittery tonight. Some day I'll tell you why. Anyway, I want to go to bed, so goodnight.'

But she did not move to kiss him. All the moves had to be his.

'Can I come in for a while?' he asked, whispering into her ear.

'No, Sam,' she said, a little fretfully. 'I just want to sleep. Don't pester, dear boy.'

'Marry me,' he whispered.

'No,' she said. 'Still no. I'm not ready.'

'Live with me, then. Be my live-in lover.'

'Sam, don't nag.'

'Why do we never get anywhere? Why do *I* never get anywhere? Nothing moves. You string me along.'

'That's not fair,' she said. 'To put it plainly, for once, I just don't happen to have fallen in love. I've been waiting— for your sake I've been waiting—and it hasn't happened.'

He drew back from her, and slouched behind the wheel again. His voice when he spoke was hard. 'It wouldn't have been like this if I'd been white.'

She turned an indignant face on him. 'You take that back! That's got nothing to do with it.'

'No,' he admitted. 'No—sorry. I spoke out of turn that time.'

'Oh, Sam,' she said, softening, 'I am so fond of you. You were sweet when you used to come into the shop and buy things you didn't need. What did you do with all that sticky-tape and torch-batteries and stuff? You are a sweet bloke, Sam, I really mean that. And you did get me out of a hole, when you talked Ken Heath into letting me rent the house. I liked you so much, I thought it would go further. But it didn't.'

'It's because I'm black,' he said. 'Because that crazy kid came out with what you're all thinkin, and ole Rastus just stood there and took it. He int a man, ole Rastus, he don't stand up for himself; he's just a grinnin, docile animal. Except at the full moon, p'rhaps, and then his primitive jungle nature come out and he go round killin people.'

'Sam—' she said.

'Well, I'm leavin,' he said. 'I'm leavin all of you. Ole Rastus done got tired of Tornwich. He's gwine back home with his pocket full of tin, O doodah day.'

123

'Going where?' she asked.

'Yas, ma'am, dat am one big question. Ipswich might not be too easy, bein as I've got the reputation of bein a triple murderer. Thass a bit too near, Ipswich.'

'You don't have to go anywhere,' she said. 'You're just bitter for the moment, but it'll pass. Not that there aren't more interesting places in the world than Tornwich. Like the Caribbean.'

'Shit,' Sam said, banging with both hands on the steering wheel. 'Oh holy shit. All you Honkies want to make me believe thass where I come from. Well, I don't. I int never been there. I don't believe I should like it. I don't want to be no foreigner. Why do you stop there, anyway, you Honkies: why don't you tell me to piss off back to Africa?'

She moved towards him and put out an arm, but he pushed her aside and leaned across to open her door. 'I don't want no white trash in my car,' he said. 'Rude woman. I done hear about you white ladies, always tryin to get into the brothers' underpants.'

She got out and slammed the door, but then appeared by his window and knocked on the glass. He wound it down, and glowered up at her.

'Sam,' she said.

'Doodah,' he said.

'Shut up, Rastus,' she said, 'I want to talk to Sam. Sam, you are a very sweet guy. No woman should be close to you—should be close if she can't be—what you need. In the end, I didn't measure up. I wish I could, but that's the way it is, Sam.'

He went on gazing at her, his face tilted. She bent and

kissed his forehead.

'Hell, I'm going to cry,' she said. 'Don't you think we can be friends, after a while?'

He lifted one hand from the steering wheel, and performed the Suffolk feint of spitting in the palm. He held out his hand without a word, and she clasped it.

'It's a deal,' she said. 'Well, goodnight, ole buddy.'

He watched her unlock her door, then close it on the light. He started his engine and moved on.

At a pub on the main road he pulled up and got out and rapped on the locked door. Presently the landlord, who was washing glasses, peered out and recognized an old friend. He sold Sam a bottle of whisky.

Harry was trying to mend a lamp which the little dog, tangling itself in the cord, had brought to the floor. Nothing except the bulb had broken, but something had gone wrong with the switch. He had it in his big unhandy fingers, trying to work out how to set the fault right.

Near his chair a fire of driftwood leaped in the grate, and polished brass winked with the flames. The cat and the spaniel, long accustomed to one another, slept side by side on the mat. Close to his hand was a glass of neat whisky. He had been attempting his repairs with a sharp-pointed knife, but put it aside, and sat thinking. Presently he placed in his mind the tool he needed, and got up and climbed the two flights of stairs to Dave's bedroom.

It was a long time since he had been in that room, and he looked around it approvingly, because it was as ship-shape as he liked things to be. Dave's possessions, which were few, were all stowed away. There was hardly a sign of him in the room, except for a framed photograph of his drowned father.

Harry gave the familiar face a melancholy smile, and then frowned slightly. The thought had occurred to him that it was there precisely so that he would see it, and feel more indulgently towards Dave as a result.

He dropped on to his haunches and peered under the bed. The toolbox was at the back, against the wall, and in front of it was a small package wrapped in newspaper. He fetched that out and left it on the floor while he dragged out the heavy box, which he lifted onto the bed.

While he was rummaging through the tools something sharp gouged his finger. He drew out his hand violently and stepped back, and the box teetered and crashed to the floor.

'Oh, shit,' he said, looking at Dave's parcel in the midst of the scattered tools. Two gashes had appeared. He squatted over it. Underneath the newspaper was plastic. He poked one of the gashes with his finger, then peered in.

He rose and stood in the middle of the floor, staring at nothing. 'My God,' he whispered to himself. 'My God, so that's it. The little bastard.'

He turned to the smiling face of the fisherman, and gazed at it vaguely.

The banging on the street door two floors below, the yapping of the dog, took a while to register with him. When they did, he gave an urgent glance at the mess on the floor, but decided to do nothing. 'Let him *know* I know,' he muttered, and went out and slammed the door.

The man on the doorstep was Black Sam. 'You, boy,' said Harry, looking distrait. 'Parky, innit?—but a nice clear night. You comin in, or what?'

'I'd like to come in for a bit,' said Sam. His speech was slurred.

'Why, boy, I do believe you're pissed,' said Harry. 'That's something I int never sin before. You lose your licence and you're in dead shtook. Well, come in to the fire.'

When he was seated opposite Harry, with the dog sniffing at his shoes, Sam said: 'You're bleedin, Harry. Your finger.'

'So I am,' Harry realized. 'Well, here's the medicine for that.' He dipped his finger into the whisky beside him, then shook it in the air to dry. Little ribbons of blood hung suspended in the glass. 'Best antiseptic I know,' said Harry. 'Can I give you one?'

'Don't think so, thanks,' said Sam. 'No, I shall give it a rest.'

'What brought this on,' Harry wondered, 'this sudden change in your sober habits?'

'Just—ah, the blues,' Sam said. 'Pissed off, therefore pissed. I saw all your lights on, and I thought I'd give you a look. Tell me to bugger off if you're busy.'

'You make yourself at hoom, boy. Look at that good fire. I'm glad there's someone here to admire it.'

'Dave not indoors?'

'No,' Harry said. 'He goo off roamin around in that van, I dunno where. Most of his dole money goo on petrol, I reckon.'

The fire caved in, and Harry got up to poke it and put on

127

coal. 'Harry,' Sam said, to his back, 'I'm in a hell of a state.'

'I believe you,' Harry said. 'You int workin, are you?'

'No, I got the day off. I started drinkin last night. I know that don't solve nothing. I know that's all there again when you sober up.'

'What is it, Sam?' Harry asked. He sat down again, but on the edge of his chair, looking into Sam's face. 'Spit it out. Trouble with Donna?'

'Yeh,' Sam said. 'That too. We int together no more, as of last night. And my job's goin, I can feel it sort of escapin from me. Christ, Harry, I don't know where to go, I don't know what to do, with this hangin over me. People are sayin I killed three people, and drove one crazy. Last night, just for a moment, even Donna believed that. Just for a moment, thass all, but after that, Jesus, how could we ever be like we used to be again?'

Harry took his eyes away from Sam's, which were slightly bloodshot, and directed them at the floor. Stony-faced, he said: 'I've heard some talk like that. But that won't last, Sam. Believe you me, boy, when they see you gooin about your daily business in the usual way, they'll start to laugh at themselves after a while. I on'y hope it weren't nothing I said that put that idea into young Greg's head. Because he's at the bottom of it, of course, but that int really his fault, bein so sick.'

Sam had sat up straighter. '*You* said something to him?'

'I might have,' Harry said. 'In the beginnin there was some talk, some theories, about you among others. And that fair got my rag out, and I might have sounded off about it in front of Greg, I don't remember.'

Sam, with a grim mouth, said: 'Thanks, mate.'

'I told you I'm sorry,' Harry said. 'Anything I said was to make them laugh at the stoopid idea. How else could I deal with it, Sam, bein on your side? I thought I was doin my best for you, that's why I spook out.'

'Yeh,' Sam said, noncommittally; but he did relax again. 'Okay. Thanks.'

'I'm a bit out of sorts tonight,' Harry said, restlessly. 'I'm a bit—whass the word?—occupied. I wish you'd have a drink. Or how about a coffee, that might do you a bit of good.'

'No, thanks,' Sam said, and stood up.

'You off already? Well, not such a bad idea. You goo and sleep it off, boy, and in the mornin things will look brighter. Like you say, the bottle never solved anything.'

Sam was at the door giving on to the street, waiting for Harry to let him out. He said: 'Things go. Like a landslide. Suddenly there int nothing left.'

'Thass the drink talkin,' diagnosed Harry. 'Very depressin stuff, if you're depressed.'

He held the door open, and Sam went out to his taxi. The light on the roof of it was turned off.

'Hey,' Harry called after him, 'smile.' And as Sam forced a grin, he exclaimed admiringly: 'Just look at them teeth.'

When Sam was gone and the door was closed against the cold he went to the hearth to warm himself. He stooped to pick up a dustpan and brush. Then he went upstairs.

And every moon made some or other mad.
And now and then one hang himself for grief,
Pinning upon his breast a long great scroll
How I with interest tormented him.

Barabas in The Jew of Malta

Now the moon is on the water, the silver-blue shallow valley to which black woods and frosty fields tend gently down.

An unsurfaced track, paler than the rimed grass, ends at the farmhouse. Its windows have a blue gleam. The rooms behind are dusty, the roof is unsound. Nobody has wakened there for years; no dog, for years, has barked at a crawling car.

He sits in the silent car which is beginning to grow chill. He watches the unstirred water. The moonlight lays a film of blue on his dark skin.

A pheasant, waking, honks in the nearby wood, and two more reply. The sound in that stillness is strident, violent. He shivers, and sits up straight.

He knows that now, after all, it will be done, that the revenge plotted in drunkenness, with anger and self-pity, will be carried out in a cold calm.

A light comes on for a moment as he opens the door, then vanishes as he quietly closes it. He has a small flashlight in his hand. He goes to the boot and opens it and reaches inside.

He closes the boot. Flashlight in hand, he squats in the whitened grass, fumbling stiff-fingered with the length of hose.

The light comes on again, and now his figure is stooping black against the door, winding down the window a crack, clamping in the crack the frost-hard hose. Then the dark returns.

The engine starts, and runs sweetly.

He lies along the seat, his knees drawn up. His hands press to his cheeks, for comfort, the collar of his sheep-skin coat. He is attached to that coat, as single men grow attached to things.

The smell from the hose was to him, when a boy, some-thing exhilarating, a perfume. It smelled of liberation and promise. His father, the black British working-man, never owned a car, never held a licence.

From where he lies the line of his eyes takes in the taller trees of the wood, sharply drawn against the light sky, holding in their black coral boughs black shocks of rooks' nests.

He is very calm. He was very calm, but suddenly his body, his heart, is invaded by a terrible agitation. His body, his shaking heart, want him to move. His violent heart is leaping.

But his body is heavy, he cannot move it. Only his lips, which open on a groan. His voice is thick with trembling and affright. 'Ah—forgive!'

6
FALLING OUT

At the top of the stairs Harry paused, holding a steaming mug in one hand, and looked across the small room to the window framing a line of roofs, and over them heavy pewter-coloured clouds with a tinge of sandy-yellow.

He stepped into the room and stood by the bed, where the blankets moulded the shape of a body. With his free hand he pulled them back, revealing a pillow and a mass of black hair.

'Dave,' he said. He gave a tug at the black beard. 'Time you come alive, boy.'

The young man rolled over, and lay blinking at the ceiling, until his eyes focused and took in the other presence. Half rising on one elbow, the bedclothes draped over his bare shoulders, he said, doubtingly: 'Harry?'

'Thass gone ten o'clock,' Harry said, disapproving. 'I brought you some tea.'

A tattooed arm came out to take the mug, but Dave was puzzled. 'Whass this, then—a celebration? Your birfday, Harry?'

'No,' said Harry. 'But thass nearly yours, come to think of it.'

'What a memory,' said Dave, but not with pleasure.

'You'll be twenty-five,' Harry said, looking down at the glossy black head bent over the mug. 'Time you was makin a plan or two, if you ask me.'

Dave emptied the mug, set it on the floor, and lay back with the blankets pulled up to his chin. 'Cor, boy, thass cold out there,' he shivered. 'Look at that sky. We shall have snow, I reckon.'

'Listen, Dave,' Harry said, 'I come up here to have a talk with you, and that int about the weather. I got serious things to say to you.'

He was looking directly at the young man's black eyes, and they showed a sudden spark of resistance, which he moved to quell.

'You know,' he said, 'I never meddle in your affairs. But last night I needed my toolbox, so I come up here, 'cause thass under your bed there. Yes,' he went on, as Dave lifted his head from the pillow, 'yes, you guessed it. What happen was, I drop some tools on that parcel and cut it open.'

After a while, Dave said softly: 'Shit.'

'Thass what you call it, innit,' Harry said, 'you modern youngsters? You call it shit.'

Dave's naked torso suddenly appeared, hanging over the side of the bed while he searched beneath it. When he came up again, the face above the beard was flushed. 'What have you done wiv it?' he demanded.

'You didn't notice, then?' Harry asked. 'I thought, when you come in last night, or this mornin, you might have noticed a smell. Because I put it on the fire.'

Dave was looking too amazed to speak.

'I don't want that kind of stuff in my house,' Harry said. 'I don't want Taffy Hughes and his lot comin in and turnin my place over. They don't even need no warrant, as I understand it. Thass been puzzlin my head for a long time, Dave, wonderin what that was what you and Frank was up to together. What I thought was, I thought that might be burglary. Well, at last I know that int—unless you got two strings to your bow.'

'Oh Jesus,' Dave groaned. 'Oh you stoopid fuckin old tool, Harry. Do you know what that was worf?'

'I don't like it,' said Harry firmly.

'You don't understand,' Dave said. 'You're too old, Harry, your generation's got funny ideas about it.'

'I was a teenager when I first smoked it,' Harry said.

'Was you?' asked Dave, surprised. But then, refusing to be deflected, he went on: 'That int no great big fing, thass just somefing people do, like smokin and drinkin. Dint you hear about that woman—respectable housewife, I fink she was—what got caught here last summer comin back from Holland wiv a pound of the stuff? She tell the magistrates: "Oh," she say, "I was on'y wantin to make tea wiv it." They give her a fine, or p'rhaps not even that.'

'She weren't dealin in it,' Harry said, 'I presoom.'

'That don't do no harm,' said Dave, brooding resentfully.

'I done some thinkin last night,' said Harry in a pleasant tone, 'and I put two and two together a foo times over. I was askin myself: Why is Linda De Vere the way she is? Why is she, Dave? What's she on?'

'On?' Dave repeated, wrinkling his forehead. 'She int on nofing. Gin and tonic, thass what Linda's on.'

'Don't push me, boy,' Harry warned. 'I'm still capable of doin serious physical damage to a soft-bellied kid like you.'

'I told you,' Dave insisted, 'she int on nofing. I fink she used to be. Not shootin up, like, but snortin and smokin. Then she got married, and I don't fink she do that no more.'

'She might have give Frank an idea,' Harry said.

'Na-a-ah,' said Dave. 'Not that sort of idea.'

'Would you know?' Harry wondered. 'When you're drivin all over the place in that van, would you know if some of that stuff you was deliverin weren't marijuana?'

'O' course I should,' Dave protested, but uncertainly.

'If that int,' Harry pointed out, 'there must be a foo other people besides Frank De Vere laughin up their sleeves at you.'

'All you're doin,' Dave said angrily, 'is makin mischief. That's it, innit? Makin mischief.'

Harry wandered over to the window and stood looking out at the threatening sky. 'Listen, Dave,' he said, 'I was meanin, before I found that stuff, I was meanin to bring you up a cup of tea this mornin and have a little chat, like. Good noos, boy. You've got a job.'

'Job?' Dave said. 'I don't want no job.'

'I know you don't,' said Harry, 'but you've got one. On

our rig, as a labourer. I was goonna ask you if you'd take it. Now I'm tellin you. You int got no choice.'

The piratical-looking young man sat up in bed, glowering with the delayed and futile rage of a rather passive child. On his chest was tattooed a blue eagle. 'You int in charge of my life,' he said.

'Yes, I am,' said Harry, and smiled at him. 'Taffy Hughes—Detective-Sergeant Lexden—them names mean nothing to you?'

He came back across the room, pausing to glance at the photograph of the drowned fisherman. He made a point of glancing at it. Then he stooped to pick up the mug from the floor. As he straightened, he gave a rough pat to the black head.

'I don't believe,' he said, 'you're seriously a bad boy. You're too gormless for that.'

He went to the door. Behind him Dave was cursing, without force or conviction, underneath the bedclothes.

In their lounge the De Veres were giving themselves a pre-Sunday-dinner drink. A pleasant smell of roasting meat came drifting in from the kitchen. It suggested to both of them a sort of sleepy domesticity remembered from other times. But Frank was turning over the pages of a Sunday colour supplement; Linda was watching the snow drift down beyond the net curtains. Their memories did not include one another.

'Don't know why we waste money on it,' Frank said at last, pushing the magazine aside. 'All that paper, and nothing to read in it.'

'I don't waste money,' Linda said, in a dreaming voice, soothed by the snow. 'I read; you don't.'

'Oh yes, you read,' he agreed. 'I can't deny that, you're good at reading.'

As she did not answer, he tried again. 'Stuffing your head round the clock with crap that's as far as possible from real life—that you do well.'

'It's not crap,' she said listlessly. 'But what would you know about it?'

'You're like a patient in a hospital,' he said, 'with tubes going everywhere. *Coronation Street* up one arm, *The Archers* up the other. Barbara Cartland up your nose.'

Roused at last, she turned her pale face on him. 'I've never read Barbara Cartland.'

'Just a brand name,' he said. 'If I say Hoover, I don't mean it's not an Electrolux.'

Her short-sighted eyes were large and vague. 'I don't know,' she said, 'why it took me so long—longer than three minutes—to see what a deeply dislikeable man you are. Last night I quite took myself by surprise. I caught myself telling Donna that I'd like to leave you.'

He asked, with a superior smile: 'To go where?'

'Where you aren't,' she said.

'I can't see it,' he said, patronizing. 'What, out in the wide world, you? You'd be like a pet hamster turned loose in an African game park.'

Then she withdrew from him again, and went back to watching the snow, examining that judgement on herself.

He stood up, an empty glass in his hand, and asked in a neutral tone: 'Your drink all right? I need another cold one.'

'I don't,' she said. 'While you're out there, baste the meat and turn the potatoes. I might not do it right.'

He went to the kitchen and took a lager from the refrigerator, and began to drink it from the can, looking out at the little yard whose high walls were rimmed with snow. The swirling flakes were coming faster and bigger. Standing close by the window, he could see two gulls wheeling among them overhead.

While he was attending to the food in the oven he heard the doorbell ring. Presently Linda called from the passage, in a hostessly voice: 'Frank, here's Dave come to play with you.'

Closing the oven, he straightened up, and looked without a welcome at Dave, whose donkey-jacket and woollen cap were white with clinging snow. 'Messy bugger,' he said. 'You're melting on the floor.'

Dave pulled to the sliding door, and then turned to him.

'Hey, what's up?' Frank asked, half alarmed, seeing the trepidation in his face.

'He knows,' Dave said, in a whisper. 'Harry. He found it.'

Frank's cold blue eyes studied him. 'Found it where?'

'Under my bed. It was an accident,' Dave explained, or pleaded. 'He bust it open, accidental, like. I couldn't know, could I, he was goonna start pokin around my fings?'

Frank said, with a venomous reasonableness: 'It *is* his house, mate. A little bit of care and forethought was called for there.'

'Well, thass done now,' Dave said, shamefaced. 'He frew it on the fuckin fire.'

He flinched a little at the fury in his partner's pock-marked face, and turned aside from the blazing eyes to find a chair. He sat hunched in his coat, booted legs stretched out clumsily.

Frank reached absently for his lager can and sucked on it.

'Okay,' he said at last, 'what's the story? What does he say?'

'Oh, he was rabbitin on,' Dave said, 'the way you'd expect. Disappointed in me, like. All that. And he says I got to start work, wif him, on the rig. If I don't, well, he kind of freatened me wif Taffy Hughes.'

'Did he, by God?' Frank muttered.

'But he wouldn't, would he, Frank? I mean, landin a couple of friends in the shit for smugglin, that int somefing old Harry would do.'

'No,' Frank said. 'No, I'm inclined to think he wouldn't.'

'So, what am I goonna do, mate?'

'You take that job,' Frank said, 'for a start.'

'Thass a fuckin awful job,' Dave complained. 'Do I have to?'

'Don't whinge,' Frank said. 'You'll do what you're told. It's not just Harry who's blackmailing you; I am too. Now, there's something I want to show you. Where's Harry now? Not working, obviously.'

'It's Sunday,' Dave pointed out. 'He's in the New Moon. He won't be back before half-two.'

'Fine,' said Frank. He opened a drawer and took out something small which he dropped in the pocket of his jeans. 'Let's go round to yours.'

When he looked in on Linda he was wearing his coat and a cap. 'Oh no,' she groaned.

'Going out, darl. Not for long.'

'We're ready to eat in half an hour.'

'I may make it,' he said. 'If not, use a bit of housewifely initiative, for fuck's sake.'

'If you're not back in time,' she said, 'your dinner will be on the doorstep in the snow. You and your bird-dog can sit and gnaw it out there.'

'If you burn it,' he said, 'I'm going to make a shepherd's pie with your ears in it. Jesus, Dave, either open the door or get out of the frigging way.'

Outside Harry's front door Dave stopped, blinking against the snow, and fumbled in the pocket of his coat.

'I'll do it,' Frank said. He fitted a key into the Yale lock and turned it.

'Hey,' said slow-witted Dave.

'I'll explain,' said Frank. He pushed the door, stamping on the snowy step, and went into Harry's living-room, where the little dog, sprawled before a dying fire, roused itself with a few yaps, but sank back again on recognizing Dave.

'How did you come by that key?' Dave wanted to know, with a censorious note in his voice.

'I was living here once,' Frank said. 'I forgot to give it back. When Harry remembered to ask me for it, it'd gone missing. But it surfaced again when it wasn't wanted.'

'What did you fink you'd use it for?' Dave demanded. 'You was up to somefing.'

'I'm about to tell you,' Frank said. 'First of all, make sure he's not indoors.'

But Harry was not in his bedroom or the bathroom, nor in Dave's room. 'Like I told you,' Dave said, coming downstairs again, 'he's always in the New Moon Sunday lunch-times.'

Frank had gone into the kitchen, and by the back door he said: 'When we go out, don't you say a word. Understand? There's half a dozen yards we could be heard from. Even with the snow, someone might have a reason to be out.'

Uncertainties made Dave particularly tractable. 'Okay.'

In the high-walled yard, hardly bigger than a room, one corner was taken up by an old brick privy, now a shed for coal and wood. Otherwise, it was bare, except for some massive and inconvenient lengths of driftwood which had been piled on the flagstones against a wall.

Gesturing at the snow-coated timbers, Frank instructed Dave to help him move them aside. They were lifted without a sound on to unbroken snow.

Squatted over the paving, Frank brushed away the cold powder which had sifted through the wood. Then he took off one glove, and dug from his jeans a complicated pocket-knife with which he began to dig around the edge of a slab.

When he raised it, Dave saw a narrow parcel wrapped in black plastic lying in a shallow trench just wide enough to hold it.

When a second flag had been lifted, he saw what the parcel must contain.

Alarm and bewilderment made him stare. Frank was grinning up at him, enjoying his face. Frank was replacing his glove. He was sliding the bundle out from beneath a third flag which partly covered it, and standing up.

The black plastic was revealed as a dustbin-liner. It fell to the snow. Underneath it was a wrapping of oily rags which, when he had removed them, were seen to be old towels.

He was weighing in his gloved hands, familiarly, with enjoyment, a .22 rifle.

Quietly he slid back the bolt and removed it, tucking it inside his belt. He reversed the rifle and put his eye to the muzzle, manoeuvring to get down the barrel a gleam of white light from the snow. After a moment he lowered and reversed it again, and replaced the bolt.

If Dave had been allowed to speak, he would not have known what to say.

Suddenly Frank bared his teeth in a grin of menace, and lunged at him, the rifle to his shoulder. Dave dodged back, but tripped on the driftwood and fell against a wall, scattering snow.

The icy muzzle was on the skin of his throat. Frank was smiling straight into his eyes. After a moment, the firing-pin clicked.

He stayed where he was, half slumped against the wall, looking on as the rifle was bound up again in its oily towels and sheathed in its dustbin-liner. He watched as it was laid again in its runnel of earth, and the flagstones fitted over it. When Frank gestured at him, irritably, to help replace the timbers, he stooped to oblige.

At the kitchen door, following on Frank's heels, he looked back and saw the fat snowflakes settling over the signs of their intrusion.

Once in the living-room, Frank threw a couple of birch logs on the fire and sank into a chair. Finding his voice: 'Thass Harry's chair,' said Dave, somehow objecting to this freedom.

'Don't let your mind stray, boy,' said Frank. 'We've got things to talk about.'

But Dave did not want to talk, and sat down on the floor and fondled the dog, which paid little attention.

'Well?' said Frank.

'Okay,' said Dave, sounding resigned. 'Tell me how that got there.'

'I put it there,' said Frank. 'It's mine.' He looked with satisfaction at the downturned face, where conflicting emotions had arrived at a stalemate, and did not hurry with his reassurance. 'But it's not what you think. I'm not the Tornwich Monster.'

Dave muttered: 'I dint fink you was. Not for more than a minute or two, I dint fink so. But why did you put that there?'

'When I was living here,' Frank said, 'I thought I needed a little hiding-place, for certain private things. I don't think he's nosy by nature, but he's likely to happen on things by accident in a house this size. As you know. So that was the hiding-place I made for myself. Not as long as that, then; I had to extend it when I used it again.'

'Why did you have it, the .22 ? Why did you hide it?'

'I had it to shoot rabbits,' Frank said reasonably, 'and maybe the odd pheasant. It lived under the seat in my van. Then, a bossy little PC hardly old enough to shave got it into his head that I was the type to have all sorts of illegal weapons stashed away. I kid you not, he was seriously interested in the fact that my old folks were Irish. So I thought the rifle had better go into hiding for a while. It's not licensed. I bought it from someone in Ipswich who'd obviously nicked it.'

Dave's slow mind was at work. 'Well, then, that don't have nofing to do wif the shootins.'

'How can you be sure?' Frank asked. And as Dave looked up from the dog, he demanded to know: 'How could anyone be sure that Harry didn't find it?'

'Ah, no,' Dave breathed. 'No, not Harry.'

'People have wondered about him,' Frank said. 'The fuzz seemed to think he was as good a candidate as any?'

But Dave had a sort of horror of the idea. 'Harry—ah, you know Harry, friend of all the world. Or wants to be. He really liked Paul Ramsey, you know he did. And then there was Ena. Ah, no, mate—thass stoopid.'

'If I accept that,' Frank said, 'then we're talking about two weapons, exactly the same.'

'Well, why not?' Dave asked. 'They int so very uncommon or hard to get. If somebody stole one and flogged it to you, that sort of prove that, don't it?'

'Maybe,' Frank said, shrugging. 'But if it was found, out there in his yard, Harry would have a hard time selling that idea.'

'I dunno,' Dave said, rubbing at his forehead with his fist. 'Yes—yes, I do know. You're goonna have to come clean about it, so they can make their tests, like, to see if that is the one, and if there's any fingerprints on it. I mean, thass what we *got* to do, even if that land you right in it. I mean, thass a dooty, mate.'

145

'He—whoever he is—would have worn gloves,' Frank said, 'that's for sure. They found nothing in Paul Ramsey's house. I don't think my prints would be on it—I made a good job of cleaning it before I put it there—but I can't be sure.'

'Oh my Christ,' Dave said. 'I never fought of that.'

'That's okay,' said Frank; 'I'm used to you.'

But Dave ignored him, and pressed on. 'If you really believe that—if you really do—I can't understand why you dint sneak in here with your key and take that away, frow it in the sea or somefing, where nobody could get at it. Just s'ppoosin that you int havin me on about this, well, then, you could have disarmed him, like, after Paul Ramsey, and them uvver two could be alive now.'

'Do you think,' Frank asked, 'that would have been a good time to go strolling through the streets with a rifle in my hand? Besides, you see, I didn't believe it at first. After Paul Ramsey, I thought: "Well, that's about the most unlikely idea that ever came into my head—but he had the means." I was just sort of playing with the idea, amusing myself. And then he threatened me. Threatened,' Frank said, jabbing at his chest with his thumb, '*me*.'

'How?' Dave asked, looking sceptical. 'Freatened you how?'

'Someone came into our house while we were sleeping,' Frank said. 'Someone wrote a note on a window, in Linda's lipstick. It said: *Not tonight—soon*. She thought she recognized my brand of humour. I let her think so: in the end, I told her it was me, getting at her for leaving the back door unlocked. But as soon as I saw it, as soon as she showed it to me, I knew who had written it. God, I can't tell you, it was like being hit in the wind. I felt him saying to me: "Look, boy, I've killed two people with a weapon that belongs to you, that probably has your prints on it, that might turn up anywhere with these prints on when I feel like parting with it. In the meantime, don't think you're safe yourself."'

Dave, painfully mulling over so many new ideas, was clicking his fingers to attract the big old cat, and when it approached began to stroke it.

'You don't believe that?' Frank asked.

'Dunno,' Dave said. 'Maybe. When you come into the Galley that night when we was there, people were sayin you looked upset, like. And then—well, like I told you the time when you was askin—he finish up his supper quick and say he have to goo hoom to watch somefing on the telly. I went to the Moon. I dint see him again till the next day.'

'I reckon he came straight back to the quay,' Frank said. 'I think he had it under his arm and down the leg of his jeans. I mean, who'd look twice at Harry Ufford, in a big old donkey-jacket, walking a bit stiff? They'd just think he was half pissed again.'

'But *you* weren't shot,' Dave said. 'The Commander was shot.'

'Just after I'd been talking to him. I'm not sure he hadn't meant to fire a round at me, as a warning. Or an experiment, to see what I'd do. But the poor old Commander offered himself, so to speak, and he served the purpose. Which was to scare me half crazy.'

Dave took that as a lightening of the conversation, and smiled. 'Did it?'

'I think,' Frank said, 'I was pretty nearly crazy for a week after that. When I came out of it, everything in that week seemed to have happened while I was drunk. Once I was sober again, I decided I'd do nothing at all, just wait and see. And everything stopped, nothing happened. I wonder why that should be.'

A sudden thought made Dave scowl. 'That was *your* idea that we should talk him into puttin me up here. That was *you* what persuaded me to stay when I was finkin of movin on.'

'I wanted an eye kept on him,' explained Frank, offhand.

'If I could believe he *was* a murderer,' Dave growled, 'I should fuckin well murder *you* for that.'

'Look, it's been like a war,' Frank said. 'I'm not particular about how I fight it. I let him see, a few times too often, that I thought he was a thick old swede. So, instead of knockin the shit out me, which has always been his way when he takes offence, he's set out to show me that he's cunning, and dangerous. Fatally dangerous.'

'I can't credit it,' Dave said, shaking his head. 'Not my dad's best mate, not Harry. He wouldn't hurt a fly, unless that drank his beer or took the micky.'

'Okay, then,' Frank said, 'have a dig around in that great brain and come up with a better theory.'

'I already did,' said Dave, glowering. 'I don't believe Harry know whass under that wood in the yard. Why should he know? I don't believe thass been moved since you moved it, until today. My feory is, somebody else see you doin that. These walls are high, but not all that high.

My feory is, someone was lookin out of an attic, or p'rhaps a barfroom window, and he get very interested in what you're doin down here. My feory is, this person is a nut-case, and the excitement of this big secret he's suddenly got is too much for him, and he finks he's just got to fire a foo shots. Thass my feory, and that make a bit more sense to me than what yours do.'

The little dog on the hearthrug woke and shook itself, and wandered over to sniff at Frank's hand, dangling over the side of the chair. Frank fondled its ears, automatically.

'Well, we don't agree,' he said. 'But if anything should happen to me, someone knows where to find the weapon.'

'There int nofing goonna happen to you,' said Dave, with a trace of contempt. 'Thass all over, monfs agoo.'

'Even so,' said Frank, meditating; 'even so.'

'Even so, what?'

'He thinks he's got a new complaint against me. He thinks I've got you mixed up in something he disapproves of, in his simple old country way. He's put pressure on you.'

'Oh, well, that,' Dave said, 'thass just doin the old family friend bit. He int goonna pass the deaf sentence 'cos of that. What we got to watch for is that he don't start whisperin in the ear of someone like Taffy Hughes.'

'Well, there you've a weapon,' Frank said. 'He's got a weapon, and you've got a weapon: the same one. But be bloody careful how you use it. Just a hint, no details. Nothing about the hole in the yard.'

'You're,' Dave said, gaping at him, 'you're so hard to suss out you int normal, you can't be. First you do everyfing you can to make me believe that the chap what sleep in the

149

room downstairs from me is a murderer, then you tell me to let him know I fink so. If I believed all your bullshit, I wouldn't never goo to sleep again.'

'There's a lock on your door,' Frank said. 'But you haven't understood me, anyway. I wasn't meaning that you should come across to him as if you were condemning him or threatening to turn him in. You'd have to sound like a friend. Puzzled, but wanting to protect him. Get him to talk about it. That'd be—oh, that'd be fascinating.'

Dave had been following intently, and suddenly slapped his drawn-up knees and got to his feet. 'Now I understand,' he said. 'We're slow, but we get there. Mrs Yorkshire Ripper, right? Brother Yorkshire Ripper, right? That's it, innit, boy? You fink we might make a fortune out of sellin our memoirs to the papers.'

'Well, it's a bit of a pipe-dream,' Frank said, 'but you make your own opportunities in this life.'

'You know,' Dave said, looking down at him with extreme dislike, 'at last you got me believin that *you* believe what you say. And it follow from that that you're ready to put my life on the line for the sake of a foo quid. You believe my life's in danger, or will be if I listen to you, and you don't give a stuff, do you?'

The sound of a key turning in the door made the partners start and turn in its direction.

'Frank,' said Harry, nodding at him. 'I knoo you was here. Linda was lookin out of her front window when I come by, and she tap on the glass and say, if you don't come soon, she say, you shall find her in a drunken stoopor.'

*

150

The snow had grown thick, blotting out the roofs of the houses across the way, and an updraught from the street tossed the flakes about crazily. They dashed themselves against the windowpane with the faintest of sounds of impact, leaving behind fuzzy stars.

Dave sat on the edge of his bed with the rifle across his thighs. He loved the slight, businesslike weight of it. Lovingly he stroked it, its slick, oil-gleaming wood.

On the floor beside the wrapping lay the grooming aids he meant to employ on it: the rags, the oil, the cord pull-through. It would gleam and become faultless from his love.

In the room below Harry was sleeping off his midday beer. When he went out again, to drink some more before his early bedtime, Dave would have to return the wonderful thing to its shroud and hide it away under the snow.

But for the time being it was his. And beside him on the bed lay two boxes of cartridges which he had found in a corner of the plastic bag. He picked up one of them and weighed it in his hand. It was full; the other was half empty. There was a satisfaction in its weight which he could not explain to himself. He opened the box, and felt again his awe at the workmanship of the marvellous little contrivances inside, jewellery in brass and lead.

The roar of a motorbike in the street roused him from a sort of trance. He bent and reached down for his rags and oil.

When Frank came home through the snowy night Linda was sitting in front of the television set. He leaned in the

151

doorway, waiting a greeting, but she did not turn. He was very used to that pale profile, paler than ever in the light from the set.

'Hey,' he said. 'How about Black Sam, then?'

'Oh,' she said, not looking at him. 'You know.'

'And you know, too. How?'

'Ken Heath came,' she said, apathetically. 'He took me to see Donna. Then he drove her to her sister in Stourford.'

He came in and took a chair across the room from her. 'What have you heard? They don't know a lot in the pubs.'

'He gassed himself in his car,' she said. 'That's all there is to tell, really. In a field near Birkness. There were some kids out enjoying the snow this afternoon, and eventually they got curious and looked in.'

'You've had too much to drink,' he said, by the way. 'How is Donna taking it?'

She said, with a shrug: 'Bravely. She blames herself, of course. She'd broken up with him, on Friday night. "Cut him adrift"—that's how she put it to me. So she's a tiny bit shattered, but feels that she hasn't the right to be.'

He got up, and took off his snowy coat. 'You going to watch that to the end?'

'I think so,' she said, indifferent.

'Well, I'm going to bed. Don't drink all the gin.'

When he was in the passage, hanging up his coat, she said: 'What are they saying in the pubs? Do they say Sam was the Monster?'

'Some do,' he said. 'Some have been saying that for a while. Which has a lot to do with what's happened, I reckon. I think, myself, Sam's the latest victim. The Monster has done for him in a roundabout way, but done for him proper, all the same.'

She turned her head towards the door with a grimace of disdain, then went back to her old movie, reaching for the glass by her hand.

I am, gay creature,
With pardon of your deities, a mushroom
On whom the dew of heaven drops now and then;
The sun shines on me too, I thank his beams!
Sometimes I feel their warmth; and eat and sleep.

Orgilus in *The Broken Heart*

She sits unmoving in front of the black and grey screen. She has switched off all other lights, and now the light from the screen, bluish, accentuates with a touch of ghastliness the pallor of her skin.

She has had all her life, though never so much as now, this look of enervation, of being bleached. Colour and energy were left out of her. What in the most vital years of her life passed for an interesting languor can no longer disguise the weariness, the lack of appetite, at the core.

She will not struggle any more against this pull on her, like the pull of gravity. There is more dignity, she has been made to feel, in surrender.

Now and again her mind strays from the images in the corner of the room to the grieving friend, and the man she barely knew. She thinks of him, so dark, lying in the fields in his white room, behind windows blind with snow.

But most of the time she lets herself be led by the hand and the eye down familiar London streets of sweating studio cardboard, through unlikely wreaths or boas of studio fog, to the recurrent meetings with a ritualized horror.

She is soothed by the formalities of this emotionless

155

dance. Grief and pain do not enter this world of screams and blood lettings.

She sips from a glass and replaces it on a table. Absently, she lights a cigarette.

On the right side of the blonde head is a white parting as straight as a ruler.

A woman of the people, drunk, goes singing through the archetypal streets, trailing archetypal scarves of studio mist.

She enters a dim archway like something on a dirty wedding-cake. From within its darkness she begins to scream and scream.

In the white parting appears a dark hole, with little blood.

After the shot, there is silence for a moment. Then, inanely meandering music, and the horrible snoring.

7

A SERIOUS CHANCE

In the mist, mournful with the sound of fog-signals from lightships and stained rather than lit by streetlamps, two dark figures advanced from either end of the street. The big-boned man in a heavy coat walked slowly and like a seaman. The child, muffled in an anorak, moved erratically, as if debating with himself whether to run, or skip, or make some sudden change of course.

'How do, Killer,' said Harry, pausing as they met under a lamp. 'That *is* you, innit, inside of that hood?'

'How do, Harry,' returned the boy. 'Boony old night.'

'Surprised to see you wanderin about in it,' said Harry. 'I believe I should have been scared at your age.'

'I int got far to go,' said Killer. 'Hey, got a snout, mate?'

'You don't smoke,' Harry objected; 'do you? You didn't ought to; you int the size of a jockey yet. Anyway, I roll 'em.'

'Thass okay,' said Killer, holding out his hand. Harry looked at it disapprovingly for a moment, then laid on it the battered tin from his pocket. The child, standing under the light, opened it and took a paper and skilfully rolled a cigarette.

'Told you,' he said, waiting to be lit.

Their two faces made a sudden brilliance in the haze, red by the flare of Harry's match. 'Ta,' said Killer, and backed towards the wall behind him, and leaned there puffing.

'I ought to be ashamed of myself,' said Harry, gazing on the scene.

Killer was showing signs of growing more relaxed. 'Harry,' he said, 'do you know where Frank De Vere is?'

'Yeah,' said Harry, shortly. 'He's at the hospital where they took his wife. Dave's expectin to drive him hoom tomorrow.'

'Has she died?' Killer asked.

'No,' Harry said. 'Least, if she have, Dave int been told. She might live a long time. Well, sort of live.'

'Like a vegetable,' said Killer. 'Int that what they say?'

'What who say?' Harry demanded. 'You ought to give them ears of yours a rest some time, young Killer.'

'Well, I just been in the Galley,' the boy said, 'seein my grandad, and people were talkin. I wouldn't want to be in Frank De Vere's shoes.'

'Nor me, neither,' said Harry. 'They on'y been married about two year.'

'That int what I meant,' Killer said. 'I mean, people are sayin he done it himself.'

'I believe,' said Harry, 'that I'm goonna have to take on the dooty of givin you a clout on the earhole; and I shall, dear boy, if you ever say that again.'

'*I* dint say it,' said the boy. 'I'm just repeatin.'

'Don't,' said Harry. 'Don't repeat it, and don't think it.'

The boy's cigarette had gone out, and as he did not care to ask for another light, he threw it away. 'All the same,' he said sulkily, 'thass natural to think it. He was in the house. There weren't nobody else there except her.'

Harry's voice rose. 'The house was brook into, boy. Whoever that was, he put sticky tape all over a pane of glass in the back door. He climbed into the yard of that house whass for sale, alongside the alley, and then into Frank's yard where they join at the corners. You ought to get your facts straight before you start accoosin men of doin in their wives—or worse than that, really. Christ, boy, if he wanted her dead, he'd have made sure, not landed himself with all this—aggravation.'

The boy was subdued. 'Sorry. Forgot he was a friend of yours.'

'He int,' Harry said. 'If this hadn't happened, he'd know that by now. But I int goonna stand for talk like that from nobody. You say it again, Killer, and I shall turn you inside-out and wear you for a muff.'

The child scuffed his feet, then looked at the man's hot face with an expression of mature regret. 'Okay, Harry. I shan't no more. But that int me you ought to be blowin up, thass the boys in the Galley.'

'And the boys in the Speedwell and the Moon,' Harry said, 'I'll be bound. All right, Killer, I'm not blamin you,

159

not really. Now you know you int so safe as you thought you was, I'm goonna escort you, like, to your door.'

'Thass on'y a foo yards,' Killer pointed out, as they began to walk back the way Harry had come. 'Thass here, look. Proper old worry-guts you are, worse than my grandad or my mam.' He gave a knock with the shining brass dolphin, and presently there were sounds of a hand fumbling with the lock. Then a lane of light cut through the mist, at its source a small girl in jeans. 'See you, Harry,' said Killer, and the door closed on him and the light.

Harry turned and continued walking towards the water. At the steamy yellow-lit window of the Galley he hesitated, making out inside the familiar shape of his crop-headed workmate, the crane-driver Charlie. For a moment he wavered, then went on to the quayside.

The estuary was shrouded, a river of cloud. But the curtains had not been drawn in the Speedwell, and at the window with a view Taffy Hughes sat looking out on nothing. His pipe was in his beard and a pint of beer stood before him. As Harry, pausing, looked in, Taffy appeared to recognize him and abstractedly raised one forefinger in greeting.

The big bar, in which several parties or reunions seemed to be going on at once, was crammed to the walls, and Harry had to wait for his beer. When he had been able to catch the eye of a harassed young barmaid, he took his pint across to the table at which Taffy sat, solitary and meditative among the standing drinkers.

'Mind if I tear you away, boy?' he asked.

'What?' asked Taffy, looking up. 'Oh, I see. Yes, I was

160

rather absorbed in my own company. Join me, Harry. There's a bit of wall there for you to lean on.'

'That bring things back to me to see you there,' Harry said. 'I see you there so often with Paul or the Commander.'

Taffy puffed at his pipe. His torso, under a blue pullover, descended in a massive curve from beard to waist. He seemed to Harry comforting, a man of weight and calm.

'Ah yes,' he murmured. 'Yes?'

'Was you thinkin about that?'

'No,' Taffy said. 'No, I was thinking of something that happened today. One of our lads turned up with an old pub sign which he wanted to hang over the door of our little bar. I had to put my foot down. The pub was called the Smugglers' Arms.'

Harry's face looked wry. 'Great thing in this life to have a sense of hoomor.'

'Do you keep well?' Taffy enquired. 'I've not seen you for months.'

'I'm about,' Harry said, 'but I get in the Moon mostly. That don't have the same sort of memories for me as what this place do. Cor, thass crowded in here tonight.' He felt oppressed by the hot bodies around him.

'Surprising, really,' Taffy said. 'I'd have expected another collapse of the trade, like we saw in November. It almost looks as if that poor girl is still not being noticed.'

'Did you know her?' Harry asked.

'No,' Taffy said. 'Who did? Once or twice I saw her, and knew whose wife she was. Sad—that was the impression.'

'Oh Christ,' Harry said, 'I hope she dies. Poor girl, poor little Linda.'

161

In the throng around, a couple of heads turned and looked at him. He picked up his mug and hid his face in it.

Taffy said quietly: 'I agree,' and did the same.

Outside the mist seemed to have grown thicker, white against the glass.

'I think I'd better drive you home,' Taffy said, 'when the time comes.'

'Thanks,' Harry said, 'but that don't matter. Taffy, I – I was kind of hopin I should see you. I looked for you, thass why I come in when I see you in the window. I thought you could—'

'You need advice?' Taffy asked, not looking at Harry, but sucking his pipe and gazing into the middle distance.

'I int sure,' Harry said. 'I'm confoosed, like. I do, but now I think that int the proper time.'

'Well,' said Taffy, 'I'm never hard to find. You look worried, Harry.'

'Thass awkward,' Harry muttered. 'Jesus, where do all these boys come from? Thass gettin hard to breathe.'

Taffy laid his pipe in an ashtray. His massive body slowly rose. 'I think,' he said, 'I'm in serious need of a slash. Hope you won't rush away, Harry.' He turned and eased his way into the crowd, which divided at the thrust of his woolly blue paunch, then closed up again behind him.

Harry, swigging from his pint pot, made a sudden decision. He planked down the mug beside Taffy's and began to manoeuvre his way through the bodies.

The door of the Gents faced the door of the single cubicle, which was standing open when Harry went in. He passed round it to the urinals behind, where Taffy stood in thoughtful flow.

'Thought it might be you,' Taffy said, turning his head for a moment, and then went back to studying the white porcelain.

Harry leaned against the tiled wall and began to roll a cigarette. 'I don't know where to start,' he said. 'I've got to be careful what I say to you.'

'Adamant,' mused Taffy. 'Adam Ant. This is where the pop-singers get their names from.'

'Could you promise me,' Harry asked, 'that this will be in confidence, like?'

'Up to a point,' Taffy said. 'But think what you're doing, Harry. I'm not in a position to promise a lot.'

'It's a question,' Harry said. 'It's what they call a scenario, like. S'poose there's this fella whass got himself mixed up in something. Something more serious than what he knoo, with people a lot brighter than what he is. S'poose he think he's dealin in marijuana, and on'y that, and the truth is his partners are usin him to deal in heroin, or cocaine, without him knowin anything about it. I know he'd be in dead trouble, but how much trouble, Taffy?'

'A junior partner?' said Taffy to the wall. He zipped himself up, sticking out his backside to negotiate the contours of his body, and turned to face Harry. 'As you say, he'd be in trouble. Very difficult for me to tell you anything, Harry, without more details. The chap—the junior partner— is a bit cheesed off, I imagine?'

'I should imagine so,' said Harry.

'Do you think he might be in a mood to cooperate with us?'

'No, I don't,' Harry said. 'Just now, no, I know he wouldn't cooperate. But like I said, he int a very bright

163

lad, this one; what he need is advice. And I don't reckon he ought to suffer too much for bein silly. Thass the others is the bad guys, thass them what ought to suffer.'

'You aren't too pleased with them,' Taffy remarked, 'are you?'

'No, I int,' said Harry. 'I int always been on the beach, you know, I sin a bit of the world. I don't like what that stuff do to young people. Thass evil, floggin that stuff to them. Thass unforgivable, to my way of thinkin. And playin that trick on a partner—thass unforgivable, too, I reckon.'

Taffy was fingering his pepper-and-salt beard. 'When you told me you wanted advice,' he said, 'I had no idea you were going to bring up anything so serious. You see how serious, don't you? I can't just forget about this, Harry. I can bide my time, but I can't put it out of my head.'

'Yeh, I know that,' Harry said. 'That just come to me in a flash, like, when you went out of the bar, that I'd goo just so far with you that I couldn't goo back. Yeh, I know you got to hear more. But not tonight, Taffy—thass enough for one night.'

'All right, then,' said Taffy. 'Well, let's not neglect our beer.'

As he moved there was a slight and sudden sound in the room. It was like the squeak of rubber soles turning on a tiled floor. Then a door banged, to be followed immediately by another.

Taffy's rather watery blue eyes looked gravely into Harry's. 'That cubicle was wide open and empty,' he said, 'when I passed it.'

'Yeh,' agreed Harry.

164

'Is that all you have to say?'

'Yeh. For tonight, like I said.'

The door banged again, and went on banging as the room was invaded by half a dozen men in blue denim. 'Gregarious lot,' murmured Taffy, navigating around them. 'Harry, I will give you a lift home, I insist.'

'Suit yourself,' Harry said, with a shrug. 'I don't reckon that make any difference. But thanks, boy, yeh, thank you kindly.'

On the winding road following the estuary the old grey van took the corners sharply, jolting the passenger. Dave, at the wheel, stole a sideways glance at him. He lolled back and stared straight ahead, looking pale, indolent.

In the winter sunlight ploughed fields, chestnut-coloured, had a sheen of barley-green. Beyond them the water lay flat as ice, and icy blue.

'Tomorrow,' Dave said, 'I shall be standin in that up to the top of my water-boots and shovellin muck. What did I do to deserve such a shit-job?'

'It might not be for long,' Frank said. His voice was apathetic, his eyes still on the road. 'What will you be doing, exactly?'

'Shovellin muck,' Dave repeated, 'like I said. Shingle and stones and such. We'll load that on the barge, take it to Gorse Creek, unload it on trucks, build the sea-wall. Harry fink the money's ever so good, he don't understand why I int chuffed about it. He goo to bed early, weekdays, and get up about four. Thass the sort of job I landed myself. So, we int had any more chats, him and me. Ah,' Dave said, slapping the steering wheel, 'I'm sorry about that. When I hear them startin to goo out, I panicked and made too much noise. They're proper hair-trigger jobs, them doors. So he know I heard him, and he'll be lyin in wait, like, to give me a talkin-to about it. What am I goonna say, for fuck's sake?'

But Frank did not answer, seeming hypnotized by the road.

'Cor, what a wally,' Dave said, trying to entertain him. 'He dint even realize Taffy Hughes fought it was himself he was talkin about. Taffy fink this "junior partner" Harry tell him about, he fink thass Harry. You got to laugh, really.'

'Not me,' Frank said. 'I don't.'

However, Dave was determined to look on the bright side. 'Look, mate, you could buy him off. People like him and my dad, they're quite interested in money, and they don't have big ideas, not at all. Yeh, I know, there's Taffy Hughes, but Harry could get round that somehow. I mean, they don't torture you in this country, they don't put you on the rack no more. That don't matter about Taffy suspectin, bein as he don't know nofing. Anyway, I int goonna be around here much longer. One of these mornins I'm goonna just jump in this van and goo.'

'It won't be like that,' Frank said.

'What do you mean?' Dave turned his head, and at the expression in the other man's set face became serious. 'No, Frank, don't keep on wiv these ideas, they're daft. He dint do it, mate. I told you, I know that.'

'How?' asked Frank languidly.

'After I cleaned the rifle—'

166

'That was a stupid fucking move,' said his friend, more in his normal manner. 'If you hadn't done that, we could tell if *he* had cleaned it.'

'Frank, that int been moved since I put that back Sunday evenin. Stoopid I may be, but I had an idea when I was doin that. After I stacked the wood the way it was, I put some bits of cotton, free freads, acrost it. They int been touched. He never had a fing to do wiv that, I'm glad to say.'

'Yes, he did,' Frank said, without emotion or emphasis. 'I know that. I know it. He saw the threads, of course he saw them. He's wary, he's canny. And I bet the crappy thriller that you got that idea from is one that belongs to him.'

'Thass true,' said Dave, a little out of countenance.

'Pull up here, will you,' Frank said, 'at the top of the hill. I want to look at the view.'

From the rise, long fields of winter-bitten grass sloped down to the saltings, and to a line of bare trees hiding a sandy beach. Dave pointed at a tall shape among them. 'Thass our crane there, I mean Charlie's crane. I went wiv 'em yest'day, so Harry could show me the ropes. I mean literally, like, show me the ropes. Goo-to-hell, boy, that was somefing cold at four or five o'clock in the mornin.'

Frank's mind was on a different tack. 'Don't you get nervous, alone in that little house with him?'

'Ah, you're off again,' Dave sighed. 'Well, I lock my door at night, since you give me the idea. But funny enough, last night he done the same. I was awake when he got up this mornin, and I heard his key in the rusty old lock. Thass a laugh, innit? He must be finkin I'll do for him before he can let it all out to Taffy.'

167

'I could guess that,' Frank said. 'That's why I asked if you weren't nervous. There's a lot more cause for it now, when he thinks he's got reason to be nervous of you.'

There was uneasy silence from Dave. Then he said: 'Well, you and me, we just don't see fings alike, mate. The way you see him, thass just unbelievable to me, and I've told you that. Less drop the subject.'

'Sure of that, are you?' Frank asked. 'Quite, quite sure?'

'I don't fink—I don't fink you're really sane about him, just now. No, I int sure, o' course I int sure, I can't see what goo on inside him. But I int scared, neither.'

'You can't see anything, can you?' said Frank, listlessly. 'You can't see outside yourself. You can't see me, and what's ahead for me. Oh Christ, I can, and I'm shaking inside.'

'I don't know what you mean,' said Dave, low.

'I know you don't, I've just said that you didn't. But I can see what's coming. I always was a bit of a favourite with our bobbies, on account of a couple of horse-pistols I owned. Now they're convinced; they're not trying to hide it; and I think Donna is somewhere at the back of this. And because I didn't do it, it's unlikely that they'll ever be able to charge me, let alone get a conviction. However, along rides Harry Ufford to their rescue. Imagine the joy at the nick when Taffy Hughes breaks the news. De Vere is nailed—not for what they'd like to see him nailed for, not for the big one, but nailed. Well, I hear that murderers have a high social status in gaol, and I suppose I'll take that reputation with me. Maybe some of my glamour will rub off on you.'

Dave was staring. 'But—that weren't all that serious, was it? Not my part of it.'

'Ah, don't go all innocent on me, Dave. It was always serious. And to get me, they're going to talk it up, pull out all the stops. Which means that for you it's going to be made as tough as it could possibly be.'

Dave's black beard moved as he munched on his lip. He was scowling, but looked more hurt than angry.

'Down there,' Frank said, 'do you see, down there, there's a bit of a roof just showing through the trees. I used to know that place well. That's where Black Sam was found.'

'Oh-ah,' Dave muttered.

'Poor old Sam. Now I know the feeling. It comes all of a sudden. It breaks like a storm. Suddenly you know that what's been threatening all your life has happened at last. For the first time, there's no choice, no way out, no hope of recovery, no free movement ever again.'

'Hey,' Dave said, and reached out a hand and laid it tentatively on Frank's shoulder. 'Hey, don't,' he pleaded. Frank's face was turned away, pressed to the cold glass. His weeping was a series of gasps of pain.

'Frank, don't,' Dave begged. 'I'll do somefing. Thass goonna be all right, you'll see. Frank, don't talk like that about not havin no free movement no more. Frank, when—when she dies—I've got to mention that—when that happen, less goo away from Tornwich. I mean, together, like. I need a partner, I'm that sort of bloke. I mean, I know I int very bright, but I've stuck to you, ant I? Bloody Tornwich, there int nofing there, never was; but somewhere else we could make somefing of ourselves, you and me.'

'We'll be leaving Tornwich, all right,' Frank said. 'For Her Majesty's Prison at Norwich.'

169

'No!' said Dave. 'I told you, I'll do somefing.'

'Have you seen a way out of this?' Frank asked. His tone was sardonic. When he turned his head, his face was strained, but calm.

'Yes,' said Dave, in a low voice. He was looking down at his hands, clasped on the steering wheel. 'There is a chance. A serious chance, I reckon. Serious.'

Harry Ufford opened his front door, and his animals, from the yard, came bursting through the cat-flap in the back door and rushed on him. He squatted to fondle them, murmuring endearments and praise. All Harry's geese were swans. They were the most remarkable cat and dog in the world, because they were his own.

He switched on an electric fire, and took off the canvas bag that hung on his shoulder, then the heavy coat. He was cold without it, but soon would have a real fire, winking in the polished horse-brasses and in the sides of bottles containing ships. He would have an hour or two of warmth and lassitude among his friendly possessions, listening to the tick of the cuckoo-clock, before the early bedtime his work imposed upon him.

He was always comforted by his house, the familiar composite smell of it. He loved the peaceful frame of his middle years.

But a thought came into his head and gave him a sudden look of sternness, a look which was always potentially there, in the broad cheekbones and lean weathered cheeks. He went to the door on the stairs, and shouted: 'Dave! Dave, you there?' When no answer came, the forbidding expression passed.

He went to the canvas bag and took out of it a bottle of whisky in a cardboard box. Looking at it, his face brightened, and he was genial once more.

From the drawer of a bureau he excavated some Christmas wrapping paper and coloured string, and on the flap of the bureau he made a neat, bright parcel of the whisky. He looked at it with pleasure. Then he went to his coat and took an envelope from its inner pocket. He produced a birthday card, and in his awkward hand wrote a message inside it.

He went into the kitchen, and opened a high cupboard, whose lower shelves were crammed with tins of pet food. Reaching high, he stowed the parcel away behind some cleaning gear.

'You better promise to be a good boy,' he said to nobody. 'Don't, you shan't have it.'

Harry stood on his front doorstep and looked at his two animals sitting gazing at him from the middle of the floor. Their eyes were sorrowful. 'I shall be back,' he told them; 'I int gone for ever.' He switched off the light, and slammed the door against their mourning approach.

In the street behind him Dave was waiting, massive in donkey-jacket and sea-boots, hunched against the black cold. It was a quarter to five on a gusty March morning.

They passed side by side through the narrow streets and narrower alleys, companionable to appearance, but awkwardly apart. They had hardly exchanged a word for two days, and could not begin to speak, with so many questions and so much pretended ignorance hanging between them.

171

On the wall at the top of Gorse Creek the slap of the low water rose to them, spiteful with wind, white-capped in the light from the waiting barge. In the blackness of land, sea and sky the little wheelhouse below them glowed yellow and warm.

By the head of the ladder which at low water gave access to the barge, Harry paused, and settled his heavy clothes around him. Clumsy in his thigh-high boots, he made his way down to the deck. He opened the wheelhouse door, spilling brightness, and said a word to the two figures inside. Then he turned back to the ladder and held it steady for Dave, who was bulkily descending.

Together they lifted the ladder down and laid it on the deck. 'Righto, boy,' Harry said, 'you lash that to the side of the wheelhouse like I shew you the other day. Thass your job now, you bein the noo boy.' He went away forward to the moorings.

When he came back, Dave's frozen fingers were still fumbling with the rope, and the throbbing, juddering barge was on the move. 'You'll get handier in time,' said Harry. 'You'll find thass a nice place, our wheelhouse, and you won't hang about out here.'

The time spent in the wheelhouse was the bright point of his working day, all that the job offered of warmth and sociability. Crammed in the fuggy stall with Charlie the crane-driver, with the taciturn Dutch skipper and with Dave's chirpy predecessor, only a few feet from the icy water, he was always in a mood to count his blessings. Though he scarcely knew the Dutchman, who lived on board, he had a fellow-feeling for the man who had made his living-quarters in the stern so snug and seemly.

The Dutchman, at the wheel, stared straight ahead; but Charlie had busied himself, and turned about holding out a mug of black coffee well spiked with whisky. 'Where's the lad?' he asked.

'He's now comin,' said Harry, and moved aside as Dave entered. Dave leaned his back to the door, and blew on his hands, slightly nodding at the crane-driver.

'He takes up more room than little Eddie,' Charlie remarked. 'We're going to have to build an extension. Here, Dave, have a swallow of something warm.'

'Ta,' said Dave, taking the mug and warming his fingers on it.

'I am thinking,' remarked the Dutchman. There was respectful silence while he thought. 'I am thinking,' he continued, 'about your police. They will take the finger-prints of all of us, every one?'

'So I hear,' said Harry. 'I hear they'll be gooin from door to door, askin everyone—every male over fifteen, that is—to report to the nick. Thass voluntary, like; but if your name int crossed off their list, they int goonna just forget you.'

'I am not in favour,' said the Dutchman. 'I am not British. Why should the British police have my fingerprints?'

'They'll destroy them after,' Harry said. 'After they've got him, I mean. It said in the paper they'll shred 'em, like.'

'After they've got him,' repeated the Dutchman. 'May we all live so long.'

'It sounds as if they've found something,' Charlie said, 'at last.'

'I don't believe that,' said Harry. 'Thass just window-dressin, in my opinion. Thass gettin them down, the rude things they read about themselves in the noos-papers.'

Out in mid-estuary the movement of the barge was unsteadying. It made him feel drowsy. He leaned beside Dave, going with the motion. Sometimes, making the trip by daylight, he was struck by the view ahead from that point, the wooded headlands so unexpectedly massive in a country which rolled so gently. That long road of water made him feel like an adventurer, perhaps a Viking, striking into the heart of unfamiliar land.

Half an hour later Dave slipped out of the wheelhouse, and Charlie asked with an unfeeling grin: 'He all right?'

'Oh Christ, yes,' said Harry, stoutly. 'He's like me, he's a fisherman's son.'

He was pleased when Dave came back looking perfectly normal, and went to stand near the wheel.

'Harry,' said the Dutchman, not turning, 'pontoon ahead. Get down and tie up.'

'*Jawel, mijnheer,*' he murmured, and went out, care-fully shutting up from the freezing air the wheelhouse's hoarded stuffiness.

He went down the two steps from the door and moved to go forward, but something caught at his clumsy boot. Something had trapped him. He felt irritation, alarm, panic. He groaned out the one word: 'Ladder!', pitching head-first into blackness.

> My soul, like to a ship in a black storm,
> Is driven, I know not whither.

Vittoria Corombona in *The White Devil*

The water is black, but pied with foam from the violent wavelets that dash themselves against his calling mouth.

His swamped sea-boots are pulling him down. He is struggling to be rid of them, trying to float on his back and at the same time free his legs of that weight. For a moment he disappears in his contortions, but when he surfaces again one overlarge boot has gone. It calms him, that success, and he works, with one hand and a stockinged foot, less frantically at removing the other. Now the weight of water is on his side. The clinging thing yields and drops to the bottom of the sea; his legs are suddenly amazingly light and limber.

The stern of the barge is going away. But they have missed him, and their shouts come to him across the waves which to them appear so small. Now he must think of the dragging weight of his coat, and he thrashes and writhes in the water, but cannot escape it. He sinks again, and comes up gasping, still hampered by the coat.

From the moment he touched the water he has had no hope, but will fight till the last moment, as a duty.

The barge has turned and is bearing down on him. It is travelling empty, and he is astonished at the height of its sides. In front of the wheelhouse, silhouetted against its light, two black figures are gesticulating.

He sees the commotion of the churning propeller, and suddenly he is in terror. He begins to shout and wave. And perhaps they see him, perhaps they make out his pale hands and pale face, because the barge veers off, the propeller merely tumbles him in its wake.

Now he tries again to be rid of the coat, and keeps on trying, but the struggle is wearying him, and again and again he goes down and swallows water.

And the strong incoming tide is bearing him away, to the farther shore, upriver.

He goes with the tide, swimming breaststroke in the freezing water. Strangely, he does not feel the cold. He only knows that he is very tired.

He feels something more elevated than self-pity. He feels grief; he mourns. It is tragic and pitiful to him that all his life—the rebellious law-breaking boyhood, truculent adolescence and man's life of loving and feuding—has been tending towards this, the death of an unwanted kitten.

The sky has grown light, traversed by long ribbons and tatters of black cloud. Now he is near the other shore, where bugles are sounding, he is amazed to hear bugles. Near this place there is a naval training school where the boys are being roused from their beds. Soon he can hear their voices, frivolous before the beginning of their disciplined day.

The current carries him on, taking another course, back to the other bank, driving always inland. Now he is too weary to swim for long, but much of the time floats on his back, paddling feebly. The lighter of the clouds are pink and golden, the black trees are turning blue.

He thinks that the craft which passes in mid-channel is

probably a lifeboat from Old Tornwich, whose crew would be men he knew. But he cannot tell, or care much, and something—tiredness or darkness or salt—has weakened his sight.

The current bears him on. His thoughts drift also, far from the river. Now he returns again and again to the disappointments of his life, the satisfactions denied, the pledges not honoured, the vague something, indefinable, sought in bouts of drunkenness or aggression and never found, always withheld from him.

He cannot tell that the lifeboat has seen him, that messages are flying through the air. Taken out of that world, he drifts.

When the barge reappears he is far from everything. He has not noticed that it is now full daylight, and that he is once more near land. The height of the barge's side astonishes and disheartens him. Hands, and then ropes, are reached down to him, but his snatches at them are feeble and unconvinced.

He sees the ladder against the barge's side, and leans back his head to look up the length of it, to the downturned solemn face of Charlie, and the face of Dave, the handsome boneheaded boy, passive in everything, a passive murderer.

He reaches for the ladder, but his fingers will not close on the rung. They open, they slip away. He drifts from the ladder's foot, and closing his eyes, goes down and breathes in his death.

8

A DEFIANCE...

'He was strong all right,' Frank De Vere said. 'What, two hours, was it, he was in the water? And he swam over five miles. Swam and drifted, I suppose. He must have had a heart like a bull.'

Dave Stutton said nothing, but got up from his chair and began to mend the fire. When he had sat down again, he snapped his fingers at the dog. It came, and he scratched the tan-coloured silk behind its ears.

'What will become of that now?' Frank wondered. 'What did Harry's brother say?'

'That'll stay here for a while,' said Dave, with his face turned away. 'I shall look after fings for him. You know, there's a lot of them Uffords, brothers and sisters. They'll get fings worked out between 'em after a while, but thass likely to take time.'

'You'll be staying on in this house, then?' Frank said.

'Yeh,' Dave said, 'for the time bein.'

'And what about the job on the rig?'

'I shall keep that, until I fink of somefing else to do.'

'That's a good idea,' Frank said, 'probably. Stick at it till the inquest, at any rate. It will look better. Though I don't know: it would sound natural enough if you said you couldn't face that barge any more.'

At last Dave looked round at him. The young face above the beard was set, and the black eyes hostile. 'No more I can't,' he said. 'However, I shall have to. I need a job.'

'I see,' said Frank, sardonically. 'Turning over a new leaf, are we? Making the clock run backwards? Not easy, boy.'

'I shall do it,' Dave muttered; and went back to fondling the dog, while the coals blazed up, the cuckoo clock, whirring, produced a wooden bird to mark eight o'clock, and sleet raked the windowpanes with bursts like automatic fire.

'You'll be going over to the old home village, then,' Frank said, 'for the funeral?'

'I s'poose I shall,' Dave said. 'Jim Ufford expect it. Well, anyone would expect that, wouldn't they?—including my muvver, I should imagine.'

Frank was meditating another question, but hesitating over it. He brought it out with caution. 'Did he know?'

'What?' Dave's face was again turned down to the dog.

'Did Harry know what you did to him?'

Instantly Dave was on his feet, and had Frank by the lapels of his coat, dragging him upright in the chair in which he lounged. 'I dint do nofing to him,' he said in a hoarse

180

voice. 'The rope worked loose, or he leaned on the ladder and brought it down on his foot. That was my fault, I know that, but thass the worst of it. So you watch your mouf, just watch your fuckin mouf, Frank De Vere.'

'Dave,' said Frank, 'let go of my collar, Dave.' His dark face was slightly darker, but his manner was calm. Suddenly he raised his right arm to deliver a karate chop, and the young man, with a hiss of pain, stepped back clutching his wrist.

'That's better,' Frank said. 'Now, let's get a few things straight. I realize that today's little tragedy off Birkness was a shock to you, and I sympathize. I know you wish it hadn't happened. But don't try to bullshit your old partner, don't tell me it *didn't* happen. I know better. I know what caused it: a halfhearted, gutless little booby-trap, that's what. And there I could recognize your handiwork: because I've never been able to hide from myself that underneath the macho disguise you are a pretty halfhearted, gutless little individual, Dave, old friend.'

Dave was mute, still rubbing his wrist, and watchful.

'That language too plain for you?' Frank enquired. 'I've always had to wrap things up for you, haven't I? But I think we might as well drop the flannel now. Why should we pretend not to know things that we know perfectly well? It's a waste of time, it's a complication we don't need.'

'I on'y got this to say to you,' said Dave in a choked voice. 'Take away that fing out in the yard what belong to you. Take that away from here and get rid of it. And give me that key what you never ought to have had. And don't you come back here, never.'

'You're throwing your weight around a bit, aren't you,' Frank said, 'for a caretaker?'

'I don't want no more to do wiv you,' Dave said. 'You keep away from me after this, or you shall be sorry.'

'Hey, now,' Frank said, and smiled up from his chair in a tolerant way, though his eyes were cold. 'You're upset, Dave. Well, I understand that, and I'm making allowances. But cool it, d'you hear me?'

He got up from his chair, and the young man, who had been standing, wavering, suddenly came to life. The punch that landed beside Frank's mouth sent him staggering back into the chair again.

'Oh, you shouldn't,' he said, looking up, pale. A little blood was running from his lip. His hands were clamped tight on the arms of the chair. 'That really wasn't clever, boy.'

'Thass enough of that,' said Dave, fiercely, though looking alarmed at what he had done. 'You int goonna talk to me like that no more.'

But Frank's tensed hands had hauled him to his feet again in one movement, and he struck out with a punch to the wind, followed by another to the head. Dave, reeling away, found the coal bucket in his path, and fell with a crash to the floor. The cat sprang up from the nearby rug and the dog yapped. All around the room little objects of brass and china rang.

Dave was gasping, and gazing upwards, dazedly, at Frank kneeling over him. 'I didn't want to do that,' Frank was saying, almost gently, 'but it had to be done. You let yourself get a bit hysterical. But it's over now, isn't it? I don't think this is quite the time for us to have a chat about things.

We'll have to, some time—but not tonight. What I'm going to do now is go out and have a few pints. I don't suppose you want to come?'

Dave, on his back, made no answer.

'I should think,' Frank said considerately, 'you'll want to go to bed now, as you're working such unsociable hours. But it's a good idea for one of us to keep an ear to the grapevine. Tell me, mate, is there such a thing as a mirror around here somewhere?'

Dave was a long time in replying, but at last said in an unsteady voice: 'Over the sink.' When he opened his mouth a little blood from his nose, invisible in the beard, showed on his teeth.

'Sorry,' Frank said, with a straight face. 'I didn't mean to hurt you.'

He went out to the kitchen, and carefully examined and bathed his cut lip. When he returned, he found Dave on his feet before the fire, his hands on the mantelshelf and his head, bowed over the glow, turned aside to a corner of the room.

'Well, I'm off,' Frank said, and opened the door. 'I'll see you tomorrow evening, I expect.'

There was a wrench of the glossy black head, and Dave was looking at him, sidelong. It was a look so candid and uncomplicated that Frank was taken aback by it, and made a movement as if to return. But the glowering, fire-dancing eyes under the black forelock presented too serious a problem. So he raised a finger to say goodbye, and went out with a bang of the door into the street hissing with sleet.

Is there a murderer here? No;—yes; I am.

Richard III

A streetlamp is fixed to the wall near his front door, and in the pinkish light the door gleams, with wet and varnish. The sleet has almost passed, but revives now and again in rattling flurries. The wind is so uncertain of its direction that a stiff piece of paper scrapes itself back and forth, back and forth, over the same short section of road.

He comes, bulky and black in his heavy clothes, from around a corner, and halts a yard short of his door, fumbling in his pockets. He is ponderous and slow tonight. He has been drinking, today and for several days, and his movements are careful, like an old man's. He is very tired. He wishes to be tired before he enters that house.

He has found his bunch of keys. They swing from his fingers.

What does he hear, I wonder, in the first instant? Something, probably, like the flight of a hardshelled insect, a zing in the air beside him. The keys clink on to the pavement, and he is on his knees, groping for them. For a few seconds his distracted face is turned full on me, whom he cannot see.

He has found his keys and is on his feet. Another leaden insect takes flight, and smashes itself against brick near his shoulder. I think from his face that he gives a sob, but cannot hear, because of the chattering irruption of a motorbike into the next street, drowning the second shot.

185

His shaking hands have found the keyhole. The doorway gapes black, then is again a gleaming barrier, on which fingertips of sleet faintly drum for a moment, close to his ear.

A RIPOSTE...

He sat in a chair in his front room, with the curtains drawn, and he was shaking. What he felt was above all amazement. Nothing that had happened in the months before, not even what had happened in that room within the week, had prepared him to entertain the notion which was suddenly a truth: that out there in the dark was a person who desired to take away his life.

In the pubs he had lately left men had been kindly with him, but guarded. At the New Moon, where old Arthur the landlord and Charlie the crane-driver had been holding a wake for Harry, there had been a reserve which he could not miss. They felt, and hardly bothered to hide their feeling, that he had never been Harry's true friend. And he was set apart by something else: not the suspicion (nothing so firm as that) but by the possibility that he was the not-quite-killer of his wife.

It seemed to him that he had been a little mad since the police had let him see that they could conceive of something so inconceivable. Then his suspicions of Harry, always real enough, though weakened by any meeting with him, had become a crazy fantasy fed by rage. He had resented Harry for years. Harry was a fool, but could not be made to feel it. When taken advantage of, he would shrug that off as a fact of life. And the respect and affection he commanded among his own kind was incomprehensible to the lone wolf. So that when Frank De Vere had persuaded himself that Harry was in every action of his life deceitful, masked, calculating and cruel, the conviction had expressed itself in him as a violent excitement. The picture of Harry (who, clearly, would be laughing) writing a threat on his windowpane was a picture that stirred him in the pit of the stomach; so cynically, so dangerously the murderer had announced himself, claiming Frank De Vere as an accessory with a sort of brutal caress.

But the game had changed; the rules, as he saw them, of the game had changed. A mild censoriousness which had always irritated him in Harry's character had reappeared; the man who had led Harry's protégé into wrong paths was marked down to be punished. And by one shot in a banal room that man had been brought close to destruction.

Only, the chastiser had not been Harry. How expertly Frank De Vere had been conned by the country boy. A few hours before, Dave had turned his head to glare at him, and he had seen in the look, besides loathing, an accusation. Dave too, he had thought, more with depression than with anger, had convicted him. A suspicion signalled till then by awkward silences had been changed (he had thought) by fury into certainty. And he had walked away from that charge with something in him like boyish hurt.

But how he had been deceived. As an admirer of duplicity, he had to admire that. He had played the fool faultlessly, that inarticulate boy with his yokel's trappings of manhood.

He could see, with great clarity, the boy-man's face in the little yard, puzzling over the rifle. Had that been another deception? He thought that it must have been, because surely Dave Stutton had found the hiding-place long before, before he lived in that house, probably on some autumn day when Harry had hired him to saw up firewood. He had seen under the wood three loosened flagstones, heard a hollowness, and made the find. With his smooth brow wrinkled and his innocent eyes wide, as at a later time.

Of course he was not mad, because madness implied excitement, emotion. What he was was preternaturally simple. Having the arm, he would go out and prove its power, always with a childish wonder in it.

Only once (thought the dupe) he destroyed with a motive. I am that motive. She will die because he wanted my whole attention.

He got up and, taking a whisky bottle from a table, swallowed a few gulps from it. Just that much he allowed himself. He had grown perfectly sober, but would risk no more.

He looked down at himself, at his clothes. Jeans, fisherman's jersey, donkey-jacket: anonymous. Men like himself walked purposefully through the streets at all hours: fishermen, crewmen from the *St Felix*, lifeboatmen. And he had a woollen cap in the hall. Fetching it, he tried it on in front of the mirror over the fireplace. With cap pulled down and collar pulled up he was concealed but unremarkable, a fisherman dressed for the weather.

He glanced at his watch, and sat down again, still wearing the cap. He was picturing the movements he would make at three o'clock. He had had, a few days before, a suspicion that the police were watching him, but a few defiant experiments he had made had seemed to disprove that. In any case, he did not care. He said aloud: 'I don't care.'

He saw himself going out by his back door, one pane of which was new glass still dirty from handling. He saw himself lithely scaling a wall, crossing a black yard, swarming up another wall and dropping into a black alley. Later there would be a few streetlamps, but he would pass under them with an urgent, preoccupied air, like a man with a cold night's work behind him and his bed ahead, face lowered from the weather, gloved hands swinging free.

At the thought of gloves he got up again from his chair. He snatched one small swig of whisky from the bottle, then went to the kitchen and began to rummage in drawers.

Methinks when he is slain to get some
hypocrite, some dangerous wretch that's muffled
o'er with feigned holiness, to swear he
heard the duke on some steep cliff lament
his wife's dishonour, and in an agony of
his heart's torture, hurled his groaning
sides into the swollen sea.

Malevole in *The Malcontent*

In the high room lamplight thrown upward from the street falls in a narrow rhombus on a white wall and is diffused vaguely into corners. The glass of a framed photograph gleams. There is little furniture. What draws most of the light is a pale counterpane on the bed, beneath which the shape of the sleeper makes a long ridge and a shadowed hollow.

It is his habit to sleep with the blankets drawn over his face. All that can be seen of him is a crest of jet-black hair on the pillow. Even if his head were not muffled, even if he were awake, he could not have heard the brief barking, soon hushed, of the dog two floors below, or the stealthy shifting of timbers in the little yard. He is dreaming; he whimpers. And the stairs are sound and do not give under stockinged feet.

The clothes of the man who comes in are a blackness in the faintly shining room. Only his hands catch the light, grotesquely bright in gloves of yellow rubber.

He squats on one heel at the head of the bed, and with great care lifts a corner of the covers. He studies the sleeping face. The lips are parted. In the earlobe that is visible is the glimmer of a gold stud.

Gently, but with steady force, he presses on the sleeper's shoulder. But the sleeper, with all the inertia of his body, resists, and the intruder draws back his hand. While he is reconsidering, there is a sudden enormous sound from a ship's siren; and the sleeper stirs and rolls over on to his back.

One tattooed arm is thrown outside the bedclothes. It is reaching, scratching. The intruder perceives that the sleeper has an erection, and wonders what will become of that, in a minute or two.

He rises to his feet and stands stooped over the bed, shifting the rifle to his right hand. With his left, softly, he pinches the sleeper's nostrils.

The head moves on the pillow, then utters a choking snore.

Now there is a hole in the black beard. The muzzle of the rifle slides into it. One yellow finger moves.

From *The Tornwich & Stourford Packet*:

SLAYER FOUND SLAIN!

'OUR NIGHT OF TERROR ENDS'—MAYOR

There was a lark, there were two larks, out of sight in a clear sky, and in the sunlight the smell of new grass mixed warmly with the cool tang of sea. Blackthorn bushes had stars of white, above yellow stars of celandine. Where the meadows ended, in saltings furred with sea-purslane cut by shining creeks, the water was drowsily blue and lulled a few swans; gulls planing over them and over the barley-green fields of the far shore.

Walking the farm track, he was restless with energies. The morning sun was in his face, and the day had made him aware of being in the very prime of life. In that weather he could not doubt that great things lay ahead for a man of thirty-four still so filled with juice and cunning.

Leaving the track, skirting new barley, he plunged into the wood. The trees above him, most of them sweet chestnuts, were bare, though hazed with reddish buds, and the

193

sun fell full on the wood's floor of grey-brown leaves and green wood-anemone, where a few white flowers had already appeared in advance of the snowdrifts which would follow.

The wood moaned and soothed with the voices of wood-pigeons, and he had an idle thought of his rifle and his marksmanship. But the rifle was gone, he would not see it again. It was stamped by the prints of his dead fingers as another man's possession.

He went on through the wood, hands in his pockets, kicking old leaves, whistling. The anemones were left behind and gave way to dog's mercury and wood spurge, the chestnuts yielded to a meaner growth in which the green-yellow catkins of pussy-willow struck a note out of place. There, where the ground was rougher, primroses were flowering and bluebell-leaves spread out their straps.

When the cuckoo called he stopped, and felt a moment of desolation. The woods were suddenly so vast, the way out of them so long. To be alone was no hardship; but who could be certain that he was alone? That very place, all country peace, had witnessed a bloody and unsolved murder five years before. While the moment lasted, he could see nothing ahead of him but a lifetime of walking past trees and doorways hiding assassins and spies: lethal tongues, condemning eyes, working, so casually, for his destruction. That, he had to believe for as long as the vision was on him, was the life of a man among mankind.

But the birds and the warm grassy air and the glimpses and whiffs of the sea turned his mood around, and the first optimism came back. Clambering down an earth cliff to a sandy beach, he felt secure again in his solitude, confident in his agility. He stood in the shadow of a tree clamorous with rooks and looked out over the flat-calm water, thinking about a second life at sea, more testing and varied than before. I will come through, he told himself. I have; I have come through.

A springlike mist hung over the town, smoky and light, at street-level scarcely more than a haze, though the spire of the church was blotted out by it. Because of the warmth of the day the presence of the sea was strong in the air, as a cool contact with the skin.

'Frank,' said the small boy idling at a corner. The syllable, accompanied by a curt nod, was a greeting not unfriendly, and the murderer returned it in the same spirit.

'Killer.'

'You're well pissed,' said the child, 'ant you?'

'Not a bit of it,' said Frank, rather testily. 'I've had a great morning in the country, and now I'm just—relaxed.'

'Relaxed as a newt,' said the boy, 'if you ask me. Are you goin to Harry's?'

'You ask a lot of questions,' Frank said. 'Yes, I'm going to Harry's. Because Jim Ufford, the brother, asked me to look after things for a while. I go there every evening, to feed the animals.'

'I shouldn't like to go in that house,' said Killer. 'But I s'pose—'

'Yeah,' Frank said, 'you're right. It's pretty much the same at mine.'

He could see the next question forming, and forestalled it by walking on. There was nothing to tell about his wife.

195

She was as near death and as far from it as usual.

But Killer, though he had given up that enquiry, did not mean to lose his company, and walked or scampered beside him, with a scuff of training shoes.

'That was something surprising,' he said, 'about Dave. I couldn't hardly credit that. I shouldn't never have thought that was someone as thick as him.'

'You watch your mouth,' Frank said, 'you little pissant. You're twelve, and he was a grown man.'

'No, he weren't,' said Killer. 'Dave was about fifteen, I reckon. Hey, Frank, is that true that he murder Harry?'

'I dunno,' Frank said. 'No one will ever be sure. But I think he was sort of hinting at that to me, as I told the law. He was feeling very bad about something. Well, that's obvious, isn't it?'

'Then Harry knoo,' said Killer, with excitement. 'Harry must have found that hidin place in the yard with the rifle in it. Thass why Dave would kill Harry; he knoo Harry was on to him.'

Frank slowed his pace a little, and looked down on the child with a thoughtful face.

'Harry knoo,' said Killer, working it out, 'and Dave knoo he knoo, but Harry dint know Dave knoo he knoo. Thass how Harry get murdered: he waited too long. But Harry would have done something, you can bet on that, a man like Harry.'

'Would have done,' Frank asked soberly, 'what?'

'Oh, killed him,' said the boy, with conviction. 'Not handed him over to the law, not Harry, not when that was Dave. Somehow or other, Harry would have killed him.'

'Here's my door,' Frank said, producing a key. 'Jim Ufford's door, I mean. Killer, you've got a mind so devious that you're practically a nut-case.'

'Can I come in?' asked Killer, wistfully. He stood for a while in the mist, dwelling with his eyes on the slammed door.

World! 'Tis the only region of death,
the greatest shop of the devil, the
cruelest prison of men, out of the which
none pass without paying their dearest
breath for a fee.

Malevole in The Malcontent

In the kitchen the animals have finished eating, and he takes an empty tin to the dustbin in the yard, which is very neat, the police having stacked the timbers once more over the hiding place, which was gaping open when they were summoned there by Charlie the crane-driver.

He goes back to the kitchen and looks at the mess on the table. Because he is drunk, has been drinking most of the afternoon alone in his own unfriendly house, he was clumsy in reaching down the tin of pet food from the cupboard, so that his fingers tangled in a cloth dangling from the highest shelf and started a landslip of cleaning gear. Now he gathers it together and fetches a chair on which to stand.

On the highest shelf is a parcel wrapped in Christmassy paper. He lifts it down and examines it.

Taped to the paper is a birthday card, which he opens, and reads:

'A drop of something to make you merry
On your 25th.
With cheers
     from
       Harry'

That brings back their voices to him very clearly. In their speech, the rhyme was a true one.

He removes the paper and looks at the expensive whisky in its box, murmuring to himself: 'I bet that didn't pay duty.'

In the living room he has a large fire burning on which he throws the paper and the card. He likes an open fire, and it is a more peaceful house than his own. He has passed several evenings here, with the animals which seem to have grown fond of him.

The firelight still shines, but more dully, on brass which is growing dimmer. Harry's presence is going from the place, from the brass and the china horses and the model ships. But not yet for a while; for a while he is still here in the room which remembers everywhere Suffolk meadows and plough-land running down to the sea.

He takes the whisky from its box and twists off the cap. 'Cheers,' he says, and raises the bottle to his mouth.

How they have annoyed me with their diversions and sidetracks leading to no development; pathological killers of time.

He switches on the television set and does not watch it. The liquid in the bottle grows less. His minutes, his hours, are like an inexhaustible flock of partridges, there to be killed, which he is there to kill.

A book lying on a table attracts his attention, and he picks it up, and opens it where an empty cigarette-paper packet marks Harry's place. It is called *The Murderers' Who's Who*, and is marked at the letter Y.

How fluid they are, their characters all potential,

veering between virtue and vice, charity and atrocity, begetting and laying waste.

The poison, he reads, was called thallium. Symptoms: stomach pains, loss of hair, numbness in the legs. In the case of one victim, diagnosed as peripheral neuritis.

But I am the end of all potential. Where change is finished, there I am inside. By me these shifting shapes are fixed. After me, they may be judged at last.

The dog yaps as the bottle is kicked across the floor. He is on his feet, but staggering. There is numbness in his legs, pain in his stomach, a formication in the roots of his hair.

He wants to run to the yard. He has thrust fingers down his throat. But terror works faster than fingers. Gasping, straining, he pukes and pukes across the floor.

The animals keep at a distance from us: silent, staring, appalled.

He lies on the floor in his vomit. He stares up into my face.

He sees me in my own likeness, without disguise. For flesh is a disguise.

He cannot speak or breathe. Yet he speaks to me, with his blazing eyes.

I can read his eyes. I have read many.

So soon? he says. *Oh, so soon.*

From *The Tornwich & Stourford Packet*:

> The Coroner was told that De Vere had been drinking heavily on that day. Death was due to inhalation of vomit.

1000 BENGALIS MASSACRED IN ASSAM

BARBIE: VAE VICTIS

BELFAST PUB HOLOCAUST

KATYN: NEW CLAIMS

MASS GRAVE FOR 'DESAPARECIDOS'

SPAIN'S COOKING-OIL HORROR

HEADLESS CORPSES IN EL SALVADOR

72 DIE IN AUSTRALIA'S ASH WEDNESDAY BUSH-ARSON

'I AM NOT A CANNIBAL' – EX-PRESIDENT

DEATH IN JOHN VORSTER SQUARE

HIROSHIMA BOMB 'A SQUIB BY COMPARISON'

All too late, all too late,
when the bier is at the gate.

Like a Thief in the Night
by Michelle de Kretser

MY COPY of *The Suburbs of Hell* (1984) is a handsome
Heinemann first edition salvaged, like so many treasures,
from a remainder tray. The dust jacket features a golden
hourglass and type on a sky-blue ground: the colours Fra
Angelico favoured for the vaults of heaven. A travel card
that served as my bookmark is still tucked away in its pages;
the date-punch informs me that I first read the book in
October 1985.

Whenever I want to re-read the novel I have difficulty
locating it. I know the shelf it sits on—not an especially
crowded one—but my eye keeps gliding past the book.
When I finally isolate it, the glorious blue and gold always
brings a little jolt. I've been looking for a black jacket, one
that matches my recollection of a devastating tale.

Randolph Stow dedicated his ninth and last novel to William Grono, an old friend from Western Australia, 'twenty years after "The Nedlands Monster"'. The Nedlands Monster was a serial killer, Eric Edgar Cooke, who murdered eight people in Perth and attempted to murder many more. In one horrific night in 1963 Cooke shot five people, among them the teenage brother of a friend of Stow's. Stow was out of the country at the time but returned shortly afterwards to a city gripped by rumour and fear. *The Suburbs of Hell* bears witness to the hold of these events on the novelist's imagination, as well as to the imaginative alchemy that has transformed a murder hunt into something far more rich and strange.

The novel updates the action to the early 1980s and replaces Perth with Tornwich, a fictionalised version of Harwich, the Essex port where Stow lived for the last three decades of his life. The small coastal town is quickly but indelibly drawn: its quays and pubs, its mediæval houses 'crammed cheek-to-cheek', its numbing cold. Secret passages designed for smugglers conjure a colourful past, fishing boats attest to a pragmatic present, while unemployment and drug dealing suggest the shape of things to come.

Stow's masterly evocation of place is matched by the brilliant economy of his characterisation. A single example will do: Eddystone Ena, who lives in a disused lighthouse, is 'a bouncy little woman, bosomed like a bullfinch'. Given the run of a neighbour's posh kitchen, she is 'delighted and overawed': a phrase that conveys Ena's modest social status, her lack of envy and her endearing readiness to be pleased—all in three words.

Like 1960s Perth, Tornwich is a backwater. In this peaceful place, a man is inexplicably shot and killed in his home one night; other murders, equally baffling, follow. For the reader, Stow's evocation of the Nedlands Monster has already created the expectation that the familiar gratifications of a murder mystery are in store: the agreeable frisson created by a killer on the loose, the smarty-pants pleasure of trying to guess 'whodunnit', and the catharsis of the eventual unmasking, when evil will be vanquished and Eden restored. For readers not conversant with the Nedlands Monster, Stow alludes early on to the Yorkshire Ripper. (The latter, Peter Sutcliffe, was arrested in 1981 after a protracted and highly publicised investigation; that Stow was moved to write *The Suburbs of Hell* soon after is probably not accidental.)

Certain aspects of the novel reinforce the reader's expectations by conforming to whodunnit conventions: the closed community; the tight-knit group of suspects; the atmosphere of dread as, one by one, victims are picked off and the noose, as they say, tightens around the rest. Even the mist that reduces streetlamps 'to dandelion-balls of light' seems to have strayed from the pages of Conan Doyle.

Gradually, however, the reader will notice an alarming thing: the police have virtually no presence in the novel. The official investigation into the murders exists only as so many noises off: the details of its unfolding, integral to the whodunnit, are suppressed. That absence is an early indication that solving the murders might not be uppermost on this novel's mind. Taffy Hughes, the sole representative of authority, is not a police officer, but only 'something quite high up in Customs'. Nor is he that figure beloved of who-dunnits, the amateur sleuth; a pipe is all he has in common with Sherlock Holmes. Harry Ufford, the novel's central character, comes nearest to fulfilling the role of detective, but it's a very approximate performance. Readers who stake their interpretative hopes on Harry will be disappointed. He displays little of the puzzle-solving acumen necessary to the part and will fall well short of masterminding a denouement. In fact, the denouement itself will fail to show.

Another break with convention is more striking still. *The Suburbs of Hell* is interspersed with brief chapters that appear to be narrated by the murderer, a strategy frowned on by whodunnit purists: it risks the untimely revelation of motive and identity, which should be deferred for as long as possible. (The ideal whodunnit is narrated by Scheherazade.) But the really unnerving discovery is that the narrator of these passages is Death itself, who follows close on the heels of the murderer (a nice literalisation, that) and records each victim's last moments with glacial calm.

The whodunnit is anchored in realism (usually, realism of the puréed, easily digestible kind, but in a way that's the point—it can be taken for granted). Stow's human characters, like their setting, are presented with realist precision; his verist rendering of the local idiom is exem-plary. The introduction of an allegorical figure—as with the absence of an authoritative investigator—muddies the novel's generic identity, causing a familiar narrative type to turn slippery and weird. The disquiet this arouses in the reader mirrors the consternation of the characters as their known world grows terrifyingly strange. Like the Tornwich Monster, whose familiar face masks a killer, *The Suburbs of Hell* has an uncanny ability to shift shape.

Nicholas Jose, a superbly insightful reader of Stow, has pointed out that his realism is always shot through with the numinous. In Stow, the divergent impulses of scientist and shaman converge (he was, after all, a poet: by definition at odds with common sense). Novels like *Visitants* and *Tourmaline* yoke a compulsion to depict the world accurately to a conviction that the world is not as it seems. The literary novel, a lively and elastic thing, can accommodate bizarre shacklings of this sort. What transfixes in *The Suburbs of Hell* is Stow's grafting of the visionary onto the calcified form of the whodunnit. That both the detective and the mystic seek the truth behind appearances seems self-evident only when it's pointed out. Fuelling Stow's imaginative leap is the kind of creative *je m'en foutisme* that Edward Said identified as characteristic of late style: counter-intuitive, intransigent, unafraid.

The title of the novel and its epigraphs come from plays by John Webster. Stow, like Webster, was 'much possessed by death', and this wasn't the first time he had turned to the playwright for an epigraph. Like the reference to the Nedlands Monster, the quotations from Webster are ominous, and prepare the reader familiar with the Jacobean stage for a proliferation of corpses.

The Duchess of Malfi provides Stow's title: 'Security some men call the suburbs of hell, / Only a dead wall between.' Perhaps the most frightening aspect of the Perth killings was that most of them took place in the victims' homes in quiet, well-to-do suburbs. People who had answered a knock at the door after dark were shot at close range; others were murdered in their beds. The Tornwich Monster, too, uses this modus operandi, one that guarantees psychosocial panic. 'Safe as houses', we say; but the security of houses is deceptive. Ena makes the point: 'When you think of your house, normally, you think of doors and windows that lock and walls that are solid. But suddenly you find yourself thinking about windowpanes that break and bolts that don't hold and smugglers' tunnels into the cellar.'

All this ratchets up suspense, in keeping with the novel's whodunnit mode. But Webster borrowed his line from Thomas Adams, a London clergyman who in 1610 preached a sermon that warned, 'Securitie is the very suburbs of Hell.' Adams' message is direct and uncompromising: wealth paves the way to damnation and death is always close at hand. It's not surprising that this sentiment resonated with Stow, a communing Anglican with a strong interest in Taoism. *The Suburbs of Hell* opens with Death quoting the Bible: 'Behold, I come as a thief' and—a verse I found terrifying as a child—'Thou fool, this night thy soul shall be required of thee.' These warnings have a worldly application in the whodunnit, but their metaphysical significance is more chilling and more profound.

Allegory, no matter what it points to, has a tendency to disturb. A refracted mode, it treats the world as a sign, always gesturing beyond the tangible. While realism deals in solid projections, allegory is hollowed out, an eyeless socket. Walter Benjamin likened it to a ruin, and allegory can feel as desolate as glassless windows and roofless walls. The events narrated in *The Suburbs of Hell* are only one source of the novel's wintry bleakness; its cold is formal and ingrained, a zero at the bone.

The novel's web of literary allusion is apparent in its liberal use of quotation. There's nothing necessarily sinister about that. But, each time I re-read *The Suburbs of Hell*, I find the presence of those quotations creepier: they eat into the body of the text like worms. If that's fanciful, it also testifies to the pervasive sense of menace generated by Stow's poetics of dread.

Stow drew attention to the novel's intertextuality by describing it as a reworking of 'The Pardoner's Tale'. Chaucer's Pardoner, an itinerant clergyman and audacious con artist, models his tale on a mediæval sermon. It was customary to enliven sermons with moral anecdotes, and the Pardoner illustrates his message that greed is the root of all evil with a story about the falling out of three 'rioters' that has fatal consequences for all three. This parable can be traced back to the *Vedabbha Jataka*, a collection of ancient Buddhist tales. Variants of the story exist in many cultures; all of them concern characters who kill each other in their lust for material gain, leaving death in sole possession of the scene.

Stow's revisioning of this classic tale is plain in the latter part of the novel, which revolves around the local drug pushers, Dave Sutton and Frank De Vere. When Harry discovers their dealing, Frank wants him out of the way. As Frank's paranoia flares, he persuades himself that Harry is the killer, a view he communicates to Dave. Whether or not Dave acts on this theory is left unresolved, but Frank later comes to believe that the killer is actually Dave. This proves to be the undoing of both men.

William Grono has said that Stow was distressed by the atmosphere of suspicion in Perth in the months leading up to Eric Edgar Cooke's arrest, and *The Suburbs of Hell* is, among other things, a study in the corrosive effect of rumour. By the end of the novel, the murderer's victims are outnumbered by those whom suspicion has killed. (Possibly not outnumbered: the score might be a draw, depending on whether one of the deaths is accidental or not.) But whatever the cause of individual deaths, Death itself carries the day.

The metaphoric import of Stow's first epigraph, taken from *The White Devil*, now becomes clear. The Tornwich killings, too, are mere 'flea-bitings' in the comprehensive triumph of Death.

While the whodunnit flourished in the interwar period, Stow composed his novel in the nuclear age, and at a time when the nature and spread of HIV was just starting to emerge in the public consciousness. Whodunnits typically offer the reassuring fiction that there is an end to killing when the murderer is caught, but in Stow's novel the killing goes on. *The Suburbs of Hell* concludes with newspaper headlines that announce untimely deaths from around the world. The narrator of *The Waste Land* famously shored fragments against his ruin; the collapse into fragments of Stow's narrative foreshadows only all-encompassing destruction. The last page of the novel features a Tarot card that represents Death—the sole image reproduced in the book.

Under that image Stow places a couplet from *Fasciculus Morum*, a mediæval preacher's handbook, where it concludes a catalogue of the physical symptoms of death: 'All too late, all too late, / when the bier is at the gate.' The doleful acknowledgment that our spiritual house is never in sufficient order echoes Adams' sermon and emphasises the moral underpinning of the novel.

Where does that leave the murder mystery? There are readers who decide that the Tornwich Monster is Death. If that solution feels inherently unsatisfying, it's because it belongs to the metaphysical order of the novel rather than to the whodunnit; it's the coexistence, not the blending, of those orders that constitutes the genius of *The Suburbs of Hell*.

Other readers buy the proposal, put forward by a child called Killer, that the murderer is Dave. But 'country boy' Dave's bewilderment when the murder weapon is discovered seems genuine, as does his instant if fleeting assumption that Frank is the Monster. Besides, Stow is mounting an ethical argument about the destructiveness of 'lethal tongues' and 'condemning eyes', and his case is lost if Killer is right. Furthermore, the coroner finds that Frank's death wasn't due to poison, but to the inhalation of his vomit. If Stow goes to the trouble of providing this information, it's surely to demonstrate that Killer's theory was only a deadly guess.

As a whodunnit addict, I can't resist coming up with a theory of my own. I think the killer is Killer: I like the narrative cheek of hiding 'whodunnit' in plain view. Here is a child who roams the town after dark, a knowing child who propagates lethal gossip, a child who, *qua* child, embodies innocence and thereby fulfils the time-honoured requirement of the whodunnit that the murderer must turn out to be the least likely suspect. It's a solution I find nifty, plausible, satisfying and laughable. The thing is, there's no solution to the identity of the Tornwich Monster: the heart of darkness contains only the absence that signifies oblivion. Stow's intelligence is remorseless here. The novel's central blank is an invitation to fill in the murderer's name. It's also a moral trap. The demonstration of our readiness to speculate and point is a form of authorial rebuke.

The Suburbs of Hell constructs a narrative as starkly simple as an image from the Tarot and as endlessly open to interpretation. Like Killer's name, it can be read literally or as a trope. But if Stow had written a conventional whodunnit that also functioned as a morality tale, his achievement would have been merely great. *The Suburbs of Hell* goes further. It subverts an impeccably contrived murder mystery, tantalising us with a question—*whodunnit?*—that it dismisses as trivial, a 'flea-biting'. Auden described the whodunnit as 'a dialectic between innocence and guilt', where the revelation of the murderer secures our disassociation from guilt. By contrast, the only 'securitie' Stow offers is none at all: the grave reminder that death will come as surely as night. One of the names given to Cooke was the Night Caller.

Text Classics

textclassics.com.au